To Cindy;

Best w.....,

Diane

D1711527

A Matter of Time

by

Diane O'Neill DesRochers

Diane O'Neill DesRochers

PublishAmerica
Baltimore

First printing

This is a work of fiction. Names, characters, places, and incidents either are the product of the author's imagination or are used fictitiously. Any resemblance to actual persons, living or dead, events, or locales is entirely coincidental .

ISBN: 1-4241-8803-2
PUBLISHED BY PUBLISHAMERICA, LLLP
www.publishamerica.com
Baltimore

Printed in the United States of America

Dedication

A special thanks to my children Denise, Joe, Michele, Rachel and Steve, whose antics and experiences became the catalyst to my writing. Also my cousin, Marilyn, my siblings, and many dear friends who offered much encouragement. Morningside Writers, Scripteasers and especially Word Weavers—many thanks for your invaluable critique, and by no means last, to my husband Joe who has always motivated me to be the best that I can be.

Chapter 1
Halifax, Nova Scotia, Canada
December 6, 1917

At twenty minutes before nine, Ted glanced at the clock tower overlooking Halifax Harbour. *That's strange, the clock is never fast.* He listened. It chimed three times then stopped. As if the stopping was an omen, a shiver slipped down Ted's back. "Aw that's an old wives' tale," he said aloud as he unlocked the door to the jewelry repair shop. "We'll have to fix it." He went through the usual routine, but with a feeling of apprehension.

His employer, Cyrus Young, was out of town. "I'll be gone for three days," he told his eighteen-year-old apprentice, "and you're in charge."

Ted checked his wristwatch—8:56. He shivered once again. *Guess I'm just nervous being in charge of the shop,* he thought and turned the sign on the glass from *CLOSED* to *OPEN,* flicked on the light switch, tore a page off the daily calendar, raised the shade over the plate glass window and dusted the tops of the display cases. Next, he rearranged several bracelets in the case and polished a ring before putting it back in its box, just as Mr. Young would do. A customer came in right away.

"Good Morning, Mr. Camden. Beautiful day, eh?"

The man shook the outstretched hand. "Sure is, Ted. And how are you?"

"I'm fine, thanks. You, and your family?" Mr. Camden had two sets of twins under the age of six and they were a handful for their parents.

"I'm doing all right and the kiddies are growing like weeds. Just stopped by to pick up my watch." He held out the ticket. "And I'd like to look at diamond earrings for my wife for Christmas."

Ted took the stub. "Of course. Right away, sir." He hastened to the workbench at the rear of the shop and leafed through several envelopes containing repaired items. *Adams: replace latch on bracelet, Brandywine: watch repair, Brown: resize ring, Camden: watch repair.* "Yes, here it is." As he removed the envelope from the cubby and suddenly there was a blinding flash of light, then a deafening boom. The impact threw Ted to the floor.

"What in the name of God…?" He crawled on his knees as the building rattled and shook while glass shattered all around him. Disoriented, the young man, still clutching the repair envelope, stood. He made his way to the front of the store where a large cabinet had overturned and daggers of glass pierced the opposite wall. He called for his customer but there was no answer. Too heavy to budge it, Ted clambered over the cabinet and found Mr. Camden lying on the floor, blood gushing from his neck.

"Sweet Jesus!" Ted's breath caught in his throat. He dropped the envelope containing the watch and rushed to the man. Remembering his first-aid class, he pressed his hand over the wound but the blood kept flowing. The fluid oozed through his fingers as he pressed with both hands. A shudder went through the young apprentice's body. *I need to get…but if I remove my hands he might die.* With one hand Ted reached up to the counter, grabbed a cloth and jammed it into the wound. In moments it was red, then the bleeding stopped. Ted felt for a pulse but there was none.

"No!" he cried. "Mr. Camden. Can you hear? For the love of God, answer me." Panic gripped Ted. "You can't die, Mr. Camden, you have a family." Ted's own pulse raced as he realized his customer couldn't answer him.

What do I do now? Daze, he picked up the watch. *I have to put this back. He can get it tomorrow.* Ted tried to clean his hands but the cloth was wet with blood. He grabbed another rag, wiped his hands as best he could and staggered outside, desperate to find help. His head spun and his feet felt as if they were of lead as he forced one foot in front of the other, like he was in another world.

The air was saturated with the sound of sirens, people yelling, dogs howling. Dust swirled along with loose shingles and other rubble. Ted brushed away a piece of paper that stuck to his face. A cloud of black smoke billowed toward the sky. The huge spiral looked like it was coming from the harbor. He wondered why the buildings across the street were flattened and one wall of St. John's Church exposed the altar and pews. Its once beautiful stained glass windows were gone, leaving ugly gaps. Another building swayed to the left, its sides buckled, the interior also exposed. Ted could see the staircase leading to nowhere.

He spied a woman lying in the street and ran to her. Most of her clothing had been ripped from her body by the impact, with only the tattered sleeve of her black wool coat still on her arm. Bending over, Ted picked up her hand to check for a pulse but it wasn't attached to her body. He quickly dropped her hand and ran to the culvert where he spewed the contents of his stomach. As he wiped his mouth with his sleeve, he saw it was covered with black soot. He swiped his hands across his pant legs then returned to the woman lying on her stomach, her face turned to the side, dark tangled hair covered with blood and debris.

Ted removed his own jacket and covered the woman. Beside the body was a tiny shoe. He bent to pick it up. "Mother in Heaven. A baby! Where? I have to find it."

He searched up and down the street. *Where are you, baby?* He crawled beneath the hedge next to the sidewalk but when he pushed away the rubble he found only a carriage wheel. Holding the tiny shoe, he went back to the woman.

"I'm sorry, ma'am. I'm so very sorry. I...I couldn't find your child." He placed the shoe next to the woman's hand then raised his tear-filled eyes toward heaven as if to pray but was awestruck by a gruesome sight. People or parts of people and articles of clothing dangled from electric wires. Some hung from tree branches like puppets. Others were in a heap on the road. Several people staggered across the street in a daze. And there were fires everywhere.

"What do I do?" Ted couldn't grasp the devastation. It was incomprehensible. He dashed back into the shop, sidestepping Mr. Camden's body and grabbed the telephone. "Operator, operator!" But there was no response. He clicked the receiver several times. "Operator, this is an emergency, I need to…"

Frustrated, Ted returned the useless phone to its cradle and went back outside. This time, more people were standing there in a huddle. He recognized Captain Mahoney.

"Captain, what happened?"

"We're not sure, son. A ship's on fire in the harbor. They think it caused the explosion. You all right?"

"I guess so. A customer's in the shop. He's dead. And that lady and her baby. I don't know what to do."

"We'll take care of it, son. I'll send someone by soon to pick up the bodies." The captain rested his big hand on Ted's shoulder. "There's nothing you can do. There are so many, and God only knows just how many, dead or injured. We can't get them to the hospitals fast enough." He shook his head. "We're trying to organize a volunteer brigade. Maybe you could help us, Ted?"

"Sure, okay, but what's the damage? How far did the explosion reach? What about my house? My parents, grandmother, sister and brothers," he rattled on.

"I know, I know. We believe the West End took the brunt of the explosion so I don't think it affected your area but I have a crew headed that way. I'll have them check on your family and let them know you're okay."

"Thanks. I tried to telephone but…"

"Yeah, the power and phones are out all over. Looks like it'll be awhile before they're back."

"I'll get my overcoat from the shop."

"Of course, but first secure the place as best you can. There's sure to be looters along when it gets dark. Where's Mr. Young?"

"He and his wife left to stock up for the holidays and to visit family in Pictou. They're not expected back until Sunday night. They left me in charge."

"Good, they're okay. Well, go back and my men will be by to pick up the body. They'll tell you where you're needed."

Ted returned to the shop and draped a large display cloth over Mr. Camden. A wave of nausea again flooded Ted's body. He shuddered and paced, not knowing where to start. His head pounded and he felt weak in the knees. *Is my family okay and, Oh God, Rebecca, is she...oh, no, the West End.* It finally registered what the captain told him. *I know Rebecca planned to stay home from school because her mother was really sick. I can't even phone her. I'll go there.*

Ted straightened up and took a deep breath to try to clear his mind as he looked around the shop. The plate glass window was shattered. It reminded him of the mouth of a monster, or the rabid coyote that came down from the mountains last winter with its teeth bared. It also brought back a scene from one day when he was playing in the back yard. Ted threw a ball but it went over his brother's head and smashed the cellar window. Only the jagged pieces remained. That night after supper, he got a thorough lesson from his Dad on how to repair a broken window.

But he wouldn't be able to repair this window because he had to take care of other things. At the rear of the shop Ted pulled out a cabinet drawer and carried it to the front. He quickly gathered as many watches and pieces of jewelry as he could. They were mixed in with the broken glass. He tried to sort them out and removed the larger pieces of glass but gave up trying to get it all. He placed the items in the drawer. Ted wasn't able to lift the overturned case but picked up scattered pieces of jewelry, carefully avoiding the pool of congealed blood on the floor. He continued to put valuables away in drawers. As he locked the cabinet he shook his head. "Anybody could get in through the broken windows or jimmy these locks but I guess it will delay them somewhat." Just as he finished, a work crew came in.

"We're here to pick up a body," said a big burly man with dirty blond hair and a day's growth of beard. Ted pointed to the shroud-covered corpse on the floor.

"Sorry about the gentleman. D'you know who he is?" asked another worker.

"His name is Basil Camden. He lives, lived on Berkeley Circle. And he has a wife and four little kids."

The man put his hand on Ted's arm. "Thanks, I'll tag him. Say, they really could use your help over on Maple Street, son. Can you go there?" The men lifted the body and carried it to the door.

"Yes," Ted murmured, taking his overcoat from the hook behind the door. He went back and pulled the shade down over the broken window amazed that the shade was still intact, only slightly tattered. Ted took another glance around the shop, locked the door and dropped the key into his pocket.

Chapter 2
Heaven Help Us

If Ted thought things were wretched on Pepperell Street, it was much worse on Maple. No upright buildings. Only the broken part of a red and white striped sign gave any indication that a barber shop had recently occupied the space. Ted wondered about the little café on the corner or the bookstore next to it. *Where are the people; are they all dead?* The place looked as though a giant had taken a rake and scooped everything into huge piles, then set them on fire.

The Search and Rescue Squad, as well as volunteers, dug through the rubble looking for people, hoping and praying they'd find some alive. But there just wasn't time to get to them all.

"Over here, son," called a worker. "Give us a hand." Screams revealed a woman pinned between the second story floor and the roof. One moment she was snug in her bed and the next she awoke to a nightmare. She couldn't move.

Ted climbed through the debris to the trapped woman. "You all right, lady? We'll get you out." Several other workers joined Ted as they strained to lift the timbers. Finally they were able to remove her and gently placed her onto a wagon for transport to a hospital. Other members of her family weren't so lucky. Three of them were crushed by the building's collapse and one bled to death from the laceration of flying glass. Ted helped carry out that body as well as others. They placed the dead in a line along the broken concrete sidewalk while other volunteers covered the bodies with sheets.

Some buildings held onto their foundations but others collapsed completely. In another section they didn't find a single person alive. Ted worked for a good part of the day, stopping only for hot coffee or a drink of water. He was offered sandwiches but the sight and smell of food was not something his stomach could tolerate. The pervading odor of burning wood, the choking sulfurous odor of coal mixed with the sickly sweet smell of burning flesh nauseated Ted. Eventually several of the wounded were extricated from the wreckage. "Heaven help them," cried one worker searching through the unbelievable damage.

Ted stopped to catch his breath. "No, Heaven help us all," he murmured.

A total of just sixteen people were found alive and whisked away to crowded hospitals. Two of the victims were children, covered with white ash, crying for their parents. Miraculously, they didn't appear to be hurt, but were sent to the hospital as a precaution, along with several elderly people. It was heartbreaking to witness such horror. Quiet tears trickled down Ted's cheeks at the pain, terror and confusion on the victims' faces.

"Need a break, Ted?"

"No. Well, yes. I'll be back. I need to find someone." Ted pulled the collar of his coat up around his ears. He was cold but not from the outside air. This emanated from within. Walking at a fast pace and with a feeling of dread, Ted headed for the West End. *I hope to God they're okay.*

He wasn't sure what to expect. That section of town was much the same as the area he'd been working in. This wasn't Halifax, at least not the Halifax he was used to. Dizzy and disoriented, Ted shook his head to clear the depressing images forming in his brain. *I have to concentrate on Rebecca, not the destruction.*

Last year while doing his Christmas shopping in Simpson's Store,

Ted met and was enamored with Rebecca but hesitated to ask her out. He was afraid she'd say no. However, one day she came to the jewelry shop and asked Ted if he would escort her to a dance at her school. Ted was thrilled. Early in the evening he polished his shoes and brushed his suit, then bathed and carefully shaved, applying a generous amount of aftershave. It stung his face for a moment. He brushed his teeth, combed his hair, dressed, then looked in the mirror and smiled. *I look pretty good, if I do say so.*

Heading to the florist to pick up a corsage, he chose a white gardenia. As an afterthought he selected a single rose for Rebecca's mother. Nervous as he approached the house, Ted set the flowers on the bottom step, wiped his clammy hands on his handkerchief, straightened his tie and took a deep breath. He retrieved the flowers and rang the doorbell on the porch. Mrs. Cranston called for him to come in.

"Rebecca is nearly ready," she said.

A moment later Rebecca walked into the room. To Ted, she looked like an angel. He handed her the corsage then held out the tissue-wrapped rose. "For you, Mrs. Cranston," he said bowing slightly.

Mrs. Cranston looked surprised. She opened the tissue and inhaled the sweet aroma of the pink rose. "It's been a long time since anyone gave me flowers. Thank you, Ted."

Rebecca removed her corsage from the small box. "They're beautiful!" She smelled the heady scent of the corsage. "Gardenias are my favorite." She blushed as her mother pinned it to her dress. Looking over at Ted she whispered, "Thank you."

Ted helped her with her coat. Rebecca gave her mother a hug and waved goodbye as the pair walked down the stairs. They had a wonderful time at the dance. Ted thought they were meant for each other as they glided across the floor. After that they dated regularly. When he introduced her to his family they heartily approved of the relationship.

Thinking about Rebecca, Ted plodded down the street toward the Cranston house. *We're supposed to go to a dance Saturday night.* Ted's friend, Gerald agreed to escort Rebecca's cousin who was visiting for the weekend but confessed he couldn't dance. *I promised I'd give him a lesson tonight.*

Rebecca had stayed home from school to care for her mother. After breakfast, she washed and dried the dishes while her mom dozed in the other room. She feared that her mother who had contracted tuberculosis would end up in the sanitarium where others suffering the debilitating disease were housed. The doctor, sympathetic that Rebecca would be alone, suggested she contact her aunt and uncle. "Perhaps you could live with them, at least until you finish school," he said.

"But that would mean transferring to another school and being far away from Mother...and Ted. No, I can't do it."

An honor student at Saint Anastasia Catholic School, Rebecca was tall and slender, with long hair that shone like black satin. Her eyes were an intense blue. Her smile exposed a dimple in her left cheek and even white teeth.

Rebecca was a sweet girl and had gone through some tough times. Her father died two years before and now her mother's illness. They lived on the second floor of a two-family house. She had no siblings or other relatives in the area except an aunt, uncle and three cousins in Moncton, New Brunswick.

She worked after school at Simpson's Department Store to help buy groceries and other necessities. After putting away the last dish, she closed the cupboard door and with that motion her whole world collapsed. Rebecca was thrown across the room against the cast iron stove as everything in her world turned black. The building disintegrated when the roof caved in and walls crumbled.

Nearing Rebecca's house Ted stopped, mouth agape. The house next door was nothing but a pile of bricks. He ran past it and saw the Cranston house still standing although part of the roof had caved in. "Rebecca!" He started to scramble up the steps and through the rubble, when a crew of workers hollered at him.

"Hey, what are ya doin'? Get out. It's too dangerous."

"I'm looking for someone. Do you know, were there any survivors?"

"I don't think so. It doesn't look like anyone could possibly survive that. Sorry."

"Do you know where they took them?"

"Probably to the morgue."

The word *morgue* paralyzed Ted. He was thinking more like the hospital, certainly not the morgue. It felt like someone had punched him in the stomach as he staggered and turned back.

The foreman stopped him. "Hey, fella, I think they were taken to the Chebucto school."

If they're at the school, they're alive! Ted took a deep breath. "Thanks." *At least there's hope. I'll go there as soon as I finish with the Search and Rescue crew. Maybe I can even leave early.*

When he got back to Maple Street, the superintendent noticed how pale Ted looked. "You okay? Did you know someone on the West End?"

"Yes, my girlfriend. Her house was partially demolished. Someone said everyone was dead but another thought they were taken to a school. How I can find out for sure?"

"There's such confusion I doubt you'll be able to find out anything just yet. Why don't you wait a day or two, there's bound to be word after that."

"But I want to go there now." Ted hesitated. "Then again maybe you're right. It is getting late." He went back to the crew. He wanted to scream, to lash out to someone, anyone. Finally he gritted his teeth and put all his energy into the work. *How could this happen?* He shook his head and tried to think of happier times to help him through the long hours. It was very late when at last the superintendent sent them home telling them they all needed a break. Ted was physically exhausted and emotionally drained. *I'll go to the Chebucto school first thing in the morning.* He slowly walked the two miles home, stunned and numbed by the momentous experience. Suddenly he thought about his family again, *My God. I hope they're okay. At least, I hope they're still alive.* He picked up the pace.

Chapter 3
My Sister

"Caroline Elizabeth O'Neill. You know it's rude to slam doors. Now reopen and close it. This time do it quietly!"

Maybe if we didn't see Mrs. Boudreau and her cute new puppy, Allan and I wouldn't be late. I didn't mean to slam the door. "But, Sister…"

Caroline never got the words out of her mouth. At 9:05 on Thursday morning a frightful explosion shook the City of Halifax.

First there was a brilliant white light, a huge blast, and next ferocious winds like a tremendous hurricane. Window glass showered the students, plaster chunks fell from the ceiling while papers and books flew across the room like deadly missiles.

What is it? What's that awful sound? What's happening? Caroline was terrified. She covered her ears against the thunderous roar and the next thing she knew, her teacher shoved her under the large desk as she called to the rest of the class, "Quickly, students, under your desks."

Sirens sounded. Children screamed. It was utter chaos! No one knew what happened. *Are we being attacked? Is it the end of the world? Is God angry at me for being late this morning? Bless me Father for I have sinned.*

16

It seemed a long time but it was only moments before all was quiet except for the whine of distant sirens. Caroline finally dared to peek out from under the teacher's desk. She looked around. The school clock, its dial smashed, dangled from the cord in the wall. Books were strewn around the room while torn pages and other papers continued to swirl about. The room was silent except for the whimper of a few students who continued to huddle under their desks. Caroline stood, still wearing her coat, her favorite hat torn from her head. A fog of white made it difficult to see with all the dust and debris. *Where's Sister? She was here a moment ago.* In a daze, the girl staggered as she called in panic, "Sister!" Dread came over her when she found the nun in a heap on the floor.

She squatted beside her. "Sister." Caroline gently shook her teacher. "Oh, Sister, please!" There was no answer. The nun's grey habit slowly turned crimson and Caroline knew it was too late. She hesitantly turned the woman over and saw that her beloved teacher was dead. Then she screamed. "No-o-o!" She screamed louder than she had ever screamed before in her entire life. And she couldn't stop.

Girls rushed to their hysterical friend. One put her arms around Caroline. "What is it?"

Caroline pointed to the floor. Another girl knelt beside the nun and prayed. One by one the girls appeared from under their desks. Most students sustained only minor cuts and all were covered with plaster dust and glass shards.

Still in shock after what seemed like hours, Caroline staggered toward the gaping hole where the heavy door once hung. Stunned, she watched as a black cloud rose from the direction of the harbor. She didn't know it was smoke. To her it was monstrous and she needed to get away from it. She put her hand to her mouth. "Oh no! Allan. I need to find my little brother. We have to go home." She scrambled over the rubble and down the broken steps to the path.

With tears staining her face the young girl prayed; for the soul of her teacher and the safety of her younger brother; for her parents, grandmother and other siblings. "Keep them safe, Lord, please! I'm so scared."

Saint Patrick's School, for boys in grades one through four, stood across the street from Saint Mary's. Caroline cringed when she saw her brother's school with its missing roof and crumbled brick walls. Desks, chairs, papers and maps looked as though someone had flung them into a whirlwind.

"Allan!" she screeched, racing toward the building.

Father McNulty appeared out of nowhere, carrying a child in his arms while herding several others. "Now, now, young lady. Don't scream. Are you looking for your brothers? The second graders are safely huddled over there and I think the fifth grade boys are on the hill." He shifted the child in his arms and pointed toward the rear of the building.

"Thanks," Caroline blurted as she ran toward the children. A group of boys stood in a circle, shivering. A few were crying but most appeared stunned and in shock. Some wore their coats but others were in shirt sleeves.

"Allan!"

His classmates pointed toward Caroline. Allan ran to his sister. She put her arms around her brother's chubby body. "Are you hurt?"

Although his bottom lip quivered he didn't speak and he didn't cry. He was covered with white ash; a dark streak down his face; coat unbuttoned, tie missing and his shirttail untucked exposing his tummy. Under ordinary circumstances Allan would have been chastised for appearing untidy. But this was no ordinary day. Caroline didn't wait for his answer. She grabbed his hand and together they ran toward home.

Suddenly, Caroline stopped. The black cloud continued to spiral up into the sky and the air was filled with a fine dust which made her cough and choke.

She muffled a scream and cried, "This doesn't even look like our street. Why are the trees bent over? The apothecary and the candy store, where are they?" She pointed. "There was a house over here. Oh, Allan, it's just too scary."

Allan didn't answer but pointed down the hill toward the water. Downtown was gone. There was nothing there but rubble, fires and a few streetcars stalled along the street. They didn't see any people.

"Where are the people? Where's Mrs. Boudreau's house? Her puppy? I want my mother!" Caroline shrieked and ran faster than before, dragging her brother with her to their home. The three-story house was still standing. *Why are the drapes closed and the windows open? It's cold out.* Then she saw the living room drapes flap in the breeze and realized there was no glass covering the windows.

"Mama, Mama," Caroline screeched as she and Allan ran up the few steps to the kitchen door.

Martha O'Neill rushed to open the door and bent to gather her children into her arms. "My darlings, thank the Lord you're home. Are you all right? You aren't hurt, are you? I was about to go looking for you." She ushered her precious children into the house.

Caroline hugged her mother. It felt good to touch her. She was warm and real. "Mama, I'm so scared. Mrs. Boudreau's house is gone. I slammed the door. And Sister is dead. Oh, Mama, hold me." Caroline sobbed against her mother. Allan snuggled against her too. After a while Caroline lifted her face and let her mother wipe away the tears.

"Dear, tell me what happened at school."

Tears spilled once more as she told her story and about how scared she was. She sniffled and caught her breath. "I just wanted you, Mama. I wanted to be safe. And Allan, he was so brave but I know he was scared too."

Martha held her children close to her bosom.

"Where's Jerry? And Charles? Have you seen Daddy? Where's Grandma? Is Ted home?" Caroline's sentences often ran together but today they were almost a jumble and her voice was filled with panic.

Heart in her throat, Martha swallowed hard. She didn't know if her husband and eldest son were safe. She said as calmly as she could manage, "Shhh. I haven't heard from your father but you know him, always busy helping others. We don't know what happened. I'm worried about Ted though. He went to the shop early today. Said something about he and Mr. Young repairing the tower clock." She hesitated, "or was that yesterday?" Martha shook her head and held back her own flood of tears. She helped the children remove their coats, dampened a wash cloth and wiped the stains from their faces.

Martha's eyes filled to the brim but she continued. "Your other brothers are fine. We brought Jerry downstairs and Grandma is rocking little Charles to sleep. Poor baby, he's been fussy most of the morning. Please be quiet. Are you hungry, dear?"

"No, Mama, I can't eat. I'm too upset to be hungry."

"Allan, would you like something to eat?"

He didn't answer but only stared up at his mother as she walked with him to the parlor.

Grandma put her finger to her lips as they entered. They could see that the baby was finally sleeping. Jerry was on the sofa with his broken leg propped on a cushion. He spoke to Allan but again the boy didn't respond. He simply clung to his mother.

Grandma spoke softly. "Children, I've been praying for you to come home safely. You weren't hurt were you?"

"No, Grandma," whispered Caroline, "we were the lucky ones. We were just scared."

Mama turned Allan toward her. "Allan, what's wrong? Why don't you speak? Are you hurt, sweetheart?"

Then Grandma said quietly, so as not to wake the baby, "Do you suppose he can't hear you?"

"Oh, my, I didn't think of that." She took the boy back to the kitchen, knelt in front of him and in a loud voice said, "Allan, can you hear me?"

Allan put his hands to his head. "Mama, there's a big buzzing noise in my head and my ears hurt."

Martha held him close to her. "There, there my little man, all will be well." She led him back to the parlor with the rest of the family.

Chapter 4
My Father

It was 3:30 in the afternoon when Jim, helped by his assistant Henry, staggered into the house battered, bloodied, limping.

"Jim darling, you're hurt. Come sit down." Martha raced to help her husband. She was stunned, frazzled and nearly fainted when she saw him covered with blood. She quickly pulled a chair out for him.

Martha looked at Henry. "Thank you for bringing him home." She looked at her husband, then turned back to Henry. "How rude I am. Oh dear, I'm sorry, Henry. Can I make you tea?"

"I really need to get home to my own brood, Mrs. O'Neill. Another time."

Jim held out his hand, "Thanks, my friend, you saved my life."

"Glad I was there to help."

Martha nodded goodbye and closed the door. She bent over Jim, gently kissed his cheek and held him close for a moment. She inspected his wounds, then called, "Caroline, come here."

Caroline nearly let out yet another scream when she saw her father but her mother put her fingers to her lips, shook her head, then said quietly but firmly, "Tell Grandma I need her, and please, keep the boys in the parlor."

Grandma put the sleeping child on the sofa next to Jerry, pocketed her rosary beads and rushed to the kitchen. "What is it? Oh my, the Saints preserve us! I'll get some bandages." She hurried away.

Martha removed the ever-present teakettle from the back of the wood stove, poured steaming water into a pottery bowl, added cold water from the tap then took a clean dish towel and dipped it into the water. She gently wiped blood and grime from her husband's face. "Tell me what happened, Jim."

"I'm not sure, but first I want to know, are you and the children all right?"

"Yes, although I'm worried about Ted. I know he's just like you, always helping someone. I pray he'll be home soon. The rest of us are fine. Allan is… well I'm afraid Allan is still in shock. He'll need you when we're through here. Jim darling, tell me what you know."

"Henry and I were taking down the boxing ring when I was buried under rubble. I didn't know what happened. We lost part of the roof and the rear wall of the arena collapsed. Luckily, Henry wasn't hurt. He saved my life. He dug me out."

"Oh my, perhaps you need to go to the hospital, dear."

"We went to the hospital, Martha." Jim shook his head. How could he tell his wife about the bodies lying in the streets, or body parts, arms and legs not even attached to their owners? How could he describe the broken buildings or the acrid smoke that not only made your eyes water but seared your lungs making it difficult to breathe? How could he tell her there were no more ships in the great harbor? How could he? How could he?

He simply said, "You wouldn't believe how many people were badly hurt in this blast. I couldn't stay. I knew you and your mother could tend to my injuries." He didn't tell her the conversation he overheard about so many people whose eyes had to be removed. He couldn't let that to happen to him. He just wanted to get home, to his family, away from the gruesomeness of it all.

Grandma returned with a bottle of iodine and an armload of linens, which she systematically tore into strips. There were several cuts that needed to be stitched, but Jim steadfastly refused to go to the hospital.

"Mother," said Martha, "get me one of my Damask napkins from the dining room."

Grandma didn't know why Martha wanted her best linen napkin when she already had a pile of perfectly clean rags on the table, but she didn't question her daughter. Instead, going to the dining room, she took one from the drawer of the china cabinet.

Martha shook the napkin out, then taking a sharp knife scraped lint fibers from the cloth onto the wound.

"This will help it to bind," she said.

When it was nicely covered with the lint, she placed a piece of cotton gauze on top and bound the injury with the torn rags, repeating the procedure on other nasty gashes.

When they were finished, Jim asked, "Can you look at my eye? It feels like I have something in it."

Neither woman could see anything in the eye upon first inspection, but Grandma got her magnifying glass and found a tiny glass shard, which she removed with tweezers.

"Thanks, that feels better," said Jim.

Martha put a patch over his eye, helped him remove his soiled and tattered shirt, discovering even more scrapes, cuts and bruises which she tended to.

Grandma made a cup of tea and added a generous shot of whiskey to the hot liquid. "Drink this Jim. It will help."

When he finished his tea, Martha said, "I know the children want to see you. Do you think you can walk into the parlor?"

"Of course, I want to see them, too."

Martha went ahead and told the children their father was home and for them not to worry when they saw the bandages. "Daddy sustained some cuts, but he is going to be fine."

Caroline rushed to her father. "Daddy, I'm happy you're safe, but you look like a…"

"You look just like the pirate in my book, Dad," interrupted Jerry. Jim smiled.

Little Charles, asleep with his thumb in his mouth was snuggled next to Jerry. Allan sat in the overstuffed chair. His big brown eyes filled with tears when he saw his dad.

Jim ruffled Jerry's hair, asked about his leg, then picked up Allan and set him on his lap in the chair.

"How's my boy?"

"I think his hearing has been impaired. And he complains of a loud noise in his head," said Martha.

"The concussion probably hurt his ears." Jim looked into his son's ears and kissed him on the top of his head. "It most likely will settle down in a day or so. At least I hope so. We'll take him to Doctor Munroe, but I'm afraid it'll have to wait a while. There are so many seriously injured people needing immediate help."

"Daddy, do you know what happened? Is it war?" Caroline asked.

"No, sweetheart, it isn't war." A knock on the kitchen door interrupted the conversation.

Martha got up. In a moment she returned, her heart pounding harder than ever. She feared she was going to hear the awful news that Ted was dead. In a quavering voice she announced, "It's Captain Mahoney of the Halifax Police Department. He'd like to speak with you."

Caroline tried to help her father out of the chair. "It's all right, Caroline. I'm injured but not a cripple. I can do it." Jim went to the kitchen and greeted the captain.

Caroline slipped back into the chair and snuggled against Allan who had fallen asleep. She tried to listen but all she could hear was her father's voice saying, "Yes, yes, I understand. Of course, let me get my coat."

Caroline slid off the chair and ran to the kitchen in a panic. "Daddy, are they going to arrest you?"

Jim laughed. "No, they aren't going to arrest me. They want to use the arena. The captain saw Ted and he's okay. Like you said, Martha, he's assisting the rescue crew. Look, I'll be back later. Meanwhile, Caroline, help your mother and grandmother. Be the big girl I know you can be." He kissed her on the forehead, then looked up. "Martha, I'll send someone over to board up the windows. We don't want to heat the entire city." He kissed his wife and limped out the door with the captain.

Within the hour, two men came by with hammers, boards and nails to block the windows against the elements. Martha made sandwiches and hot tea spiked with her husband's whiskey and fed the men. With the windows boarded, the house was in complete darkness. They lit kerosene lamps and awaited an uncertain future.

Chapter 5
Suppertime

"Caroline, set the table please."

"Okay. Something smells yummy. Are you making Welsh rarebit?"

"Yes, and I hope you'll be able to eat now."

"I think so. I'm hungry. Grandma, do you suppose we'll feel safe ever again? I'm still very shaky."

"Of course you're shaky. I can't imagine how awful it was for you today."

"It was horrible. Was it bad here too?"

"We were pretty frightened when the house shook and the windows shattered. We didn't know what happened."

"I thought it was the end of the world. I thought God was mad at me for being late for school."

"You were late?"

"Mrs. Boudreau was walking her new puppy. Oh, Grandma, you have to see how cute the little dog is. I hope it's okay. The Boudreau house is a wreck."

"Your mother checked on Mrs. Boudreau who was taken to the hospital. They think she may have a broken hip."

"Oh my. But what about the puppy, I wonder?"

"I don't know. Ask your mother, she probably knows."

"Okay. Should I set places for Our Father and Ted?"

Grandma smiled. Caroline often referred to Jim as Our Father. "I don't know. Why yes, of course. Set a place for both of them."

Martha woke the baby, changed his diaper, put him in the high chair and handed him a soda cracker to nibble while supper was being prepared. Allan and Jerry came to the table.

Caroline gave Allan a cracker and a quick kiss on the cheek. He smiled a crooked little grin. It felt good to see her usually happy brother smile.

As they sat around the table Caroline asked. "What do you suppose happened today? I don't understand how a fire in the harbor could wreck the whole city."

"Well, it certainly was *loud* enough to wreck the whole city," said Jerry.

"We still don't know what really happened but I'm sure we'll find out soon enough." Martha hesitated. "We won't wait for Daddy or Ted but we should thank the Lord for keeping our family safe. Let's bow our heads."

Martha recited, "Bless us, oh Lord for these thy gifts, which we are about to receive from thy bounty through Christ our Lord."

In unison they chorused, "Amen."

"'Men!" Charles repeated in a big voice. The children giggled.

Mama handed the plates to Grandma who ladled the rich creamy cheese sauce over the cracker-lined plates and put one in front of each child. Next, she broke crackers into a small bowl and poured rarebit on top. Taking a small spoonful, Martha blew on it to cool the cheese before feeding it to the baby. He was ravenous and gobbled it down.

The children were hungry and the light supper appealed to them. It was their favorite meal, usually reserved for Sunday nights but Grandma thought it was appropriate tonight.

When Martha was finished she brought her dish and the baby's to the sink.

"I'll clean up, Martha, you have things to do."

"Thank you, Mother, I appreciate it. Caroline, when you're through I want you to help me upstairs."

The second floor was in complete disarray. Glass and wood splinters were piled near each of the windows. Martha swept while Caroline held the kerosene lamp. Then, together they pulled several mattresses from the beds, carried them to the staircase and let them slide down. At the bottom, they dragged the mattresses into the parlor and put clean sheets and quilts on them to make up the beds.

"We'll sleep here tonight," said Martha.

"Yippee," squealed Jerry. "Sounds like fun."

"It will be cozy but I don't want any horseplay. How does your leg feel, dear?"

"It feels good, Mama. When will I get the cast off? I want to go to school and see my friends."

Caroline interjected. "I don't think there'll be school for a while and I doubt you'll be able to climb the big tree you fell from ever again because it's…well it's gone."

"Gone?"

"Yes, gone. Practically all the trees on Robie Street are down. It's dreadful."

"Really? Our house shook and creaked and the wind blew and windows broke. It was scary. We didn't know what happened. At first, Grandma thought it was an earthquake but I guess it wasn't. We huddled together in the closet under the staircase. Mama was worried about you and Allan. We were all scared, but I think I was the scaredest. Did your teacher really die?"

"Most scared," corrected Caroline, "and yes she did. It was gruesome, all that blood. Oh let's not talk about it, we'll have nightmares." Caroline helped the boys get ready for bed. Martha listened to their prayers and tucked them in.

"G'night," said Caroline.

"Sleep tight," chimed Jerry.

"Don't let the bedbugs bite!" Caroline giggled as she scooted from the room.

Martha called after her. "Caroline, you need a bath. Ask Grandma to heat the water."

"Okay, Mama." Caroline went to the kitchen. "Mama says I have to take a bath. Would you please heat the water for me?"

"Of course, dear," said Grandma, drying her hands and lighting the hot water heater. "I agree with your mother, you do need a bath, and a shampoo." She picked a piece of plaster from the girl's hair, then handed her a kerosene lamp. "I think you'll feel better too."

"Thanks, Grandma." Caroline reached for the lamp and climbed the stairs to her room. Opening her dresser drawer, she removed clean pajamas and underwear, As she approached the closet, she noticed her framed sampler on the floor.

Picking it up, she blew off the plaster dust and held it to her chest for a moment before setting it on her bedside table. "I love this frame," Caroline whispered to herself. "Daddy made it. Grandma helped me with the French knots on the sampler. Sister expected them to be perfect or we had to redo them."

Caroline reached in the closet for her robe and slippers. "Poor Sister. I should have gone to my own desk, then maybe she'd have been safe. Can't believe she's really dead. What was I thinking, running off like that? But I had to get Allan. I know he was scared to death. Oops, I shouldn't say or even think that." She wiped her tears. *My heart beats so fast when I think about today. It has to be the worst day of my entire life.* "It's just too awful!" She sobbed then quickly grabbed the rest of her things, descended the stairs and went into the bathroom. Setting the lamp on top of the commode, Caroline inhaled the sweet and steamy smell of the bath.

As she removed her clothing, she noted the bubbles in the tub. *Grandma, you used the bubble bath Ted bought you for Christmas.* The water felt silky and warm and the young girl sank into it. Exhausted, her mind wandered as she thought of the sampler and frame, her teacher and the destruction. Caroline wept again, then with a vengeance, picked up the washcloth and scrubbed her face and body. She shampooed her hair, rinsing it under the faucet.

How quickly things change. Not long ago we were a happy-go-lucky family. Last week we went sledding on Citadel Hill, all except Grandma and the baby. We had so much fun. Daddy and Ted pulled the sleds up the hill. At the top we could see over the entire City of Halifax right down to the water. The beautiful waterfront, the shops, the streetcars and all the ships in the harbor. All are gone now.

"Caroline, are you nearly finished?"Again, the girl was brought back to reality by her mother calling.

"I'm getting out now, Mama." Wringing out the washcloth, she put it to her face once more and inhaled the sweet scent of the soap and bubble bath. *Grandma was right. I do feel better.* Emerging from the tub, Caroline dried herself, patted sweet-smelling talcum all over before donning pajamas, robe and slippers. Then she combed her hair and brushed her teeth.

Caroline stood next to the kitchen stove to dry her hair before bidding, "Goodnight, Mama. Goodnight, Grandma and thank you for the bubble bath." She gave the women hugs and kisses then crawled onto a mattress and pulled up the quilt.

Caroline soon fell asleep but sleep was not peaceful. She dreamed of running from place to place and of things falling on top of her. She heard the screams, saw the blood, smelled the smoke and at one point cried out. Grandma put her arm across her granddaughter's slender body to calm the frightened girl.

Chapter 6
Father and Son

Ted stumbled through the dark to the door, his face ashen, clothing disheveled and bloody. Rushing to her eldest son, Martha gulped, "My God Ted, you're hurt!"

Caroline heard her brother come in and jumped out of bed. A chill came over her. She started into the kitchen ready to bombard him with questions about what happened and where he was when the blast occurred but stopped in the doorway when she saw him speak with their mother, then put his head in his hands and sob. Tears came to her own eyes when she saw his bloodstained clothing and knew he'd seen more than she wanted to know. She scurried back to the parlor, crawled under the blankets and snuggled against her grandmother.

"No, Mother," said Ted. "I'm not hurt. I was most fortunate. However, Mr. Camden wasn't. He came for his watch. I went in the back to get it when the explosion occurred. Poor man didn't have a chance standing beside the plate glass window." Ted's eyes were red and tear-filled. "Captain Mahoney asked me to help with the search and rescue. Oh, Mama, we saw so many people, it was horrifying! I wanted to find Rebecca but her whole neighborhood was completely destroyed. There was not much left of her house. I couldn't find her.

I'm worried. It doesn't look good." Ted broke down and wept, his head in his hands.

Martha didn't say anything. She couldn't. The lump in her own throat kept her from speaking. She put her arm around her son and let him weep. Then her natural motherly instinct took over. "Can I fix you a cup of tea, Ted, or something to eat?"

Ted shook his head. "I can't eat."

Martha told him about their day and how the family was scared but safe even though his father suffered injuries. "Captain Mahoney came by. He told us you were okay and asked to use the arena. Dad's there now."

Ted retrieved his coat. "Yes, he said he'd get word to you. I'll go help Dad." Ted hugged his mother as he went out the door.

The arena was just two blocks from the house. There were still smoldering embers where buildings once stood. The acrid smell in the air caused Ted to cough. As he walked up the steps to the arena and opened the door, it was quiet and all seemed fine at first. Then he saw the bodies. Some were covered with sheets and placed in a row along the floor of the arena, like on Maple Street. Others were merely left at the door. Nauseated, Ted raced for the bathroom. When the retching finally subsided, he splashed water on his face, took a deep breath and returned to his dad.

"You all right?"

"I guess. Glad our family's okay. I'm worried about Rebecca though. She wasn't at her house. I couldn't find out anything. Dad, what should I do? I want to find her before it's too late but there just doesn't seem to be enough time."

Jim put his arm around his son's shoulders. "I don't think there's anything you can do at the moment. I think you just have to wait it out. She's probably at the hospital with her mother. You said Mrs. Cranston was ill."

"You're right. At least I hope you are." Ted wasn't emotionally prepared to see people identifying members of their families. They'd ask: "Did you see my wife?" "Have you seen my son?" "I'm looking for my children." Some bodies were identified but others weren't because entire families were wiped out. There simply was no one left to claim them. However, when they did find a relative it was crushing to hear them wail and sob while holding and kissing the broken bodies of their loved ones. One man discovered his wife and their infant son. He clung to them, cradling both to his chest. "Why, oh God, why?"

When at last there was a break Ted said, "It's been a hell of a day, Dad. Like a nightmare. Mother told me how Henry saved your life. You okay?"

Jim chuckled nervously. "I thought I was a goner. However, Henry came through. I don't know how he did it by himself but he managed to pull the heavy beams, shingles and boards off me."

"Good old Henry, always there, eh? But you sure have a lot of bandages. What happened?"

"I'm fine. Just a few scratches is all."

"You sure?"

Jim nodded.

"Will they be able to repair the arena, Dad?"

"I feel certain we can fix it. Just as soon as supplies are available we'll have it up and running. After all, hockey season starts in two weeks."

Jim would never forget this day as long as he lived. As caretaker of the skating arena, he and his assistant were busy taking down the boxing ring when the explosion occurred, collapsing the wall and burying Jim in the ruins. With the strength of a giant, Henry somehow dug him out. He first thought Jim, unconscious and covered with blood, was dead but he regained consciousness as Henry extricated him from the debris.

"My God, Jim, I don't know what happened but we need to get you to the hospital right away. I'll see if I can find someone to help us."

Jim struggled to push some of the rubble away. "Damn, it hurts!" He wiped his face several times trying to clear his head and especially his eye; everything was bloody.

Henry returned with two men who helped carry Jim out of the building.

"Do you know what caused the blast?" Henry asked the men.

"No, but it sure was a hell of an explosion, I tell you," said one.

A horse and buggy sat idle on the street, the driver slumped over. Henry checked on the man. "Get this guy in the back and we'll take both men to the hospital," he ordered then hopped into the driver's seat. They had to detour around overturned streetcars, as well as the unending piles of rubble but they managed to get through.

Chaos filled the hospital. Medical assistants rushed the injured driver onto a stretcher and carried him inside. By this time Jim, although wobbly, could walk. Henry helped him through the door. Jim's eyesight was blurry, his head ached and he felt faint. The place was a beehive of activity and to him, it sounded like hundreds of people screaming in pain. He overheard a nurse talking to another as they hurried by, "They've removed many eyes imbedded with shards of glass. It's horrific. I imagine the count will go up considerably."

Jim panicked. "Let's get the hell out of here. Help me back to my house, Henry. I'm not hurt nearly as bad as these people. Please, take me home."

"I know what you mean." Henry had also heard the conversation. Once outside they discovered their horse and buggy missing, but another empty one was nearby. Henry helped Jim into the back and they headed for the O'Neill house.

I pray to God my family is safe. Don't know what I'd do it if anything happened to them. They mean the world to me. Merciful sleep closed Jim's eyes.

Chapter 7
My Mother

She paced back and forth in the kitchen during the early morning. Neither Jim nor Ted had come home during the night. Martha was worried. Finally, she put on her winter coat, wrapped a scarf around her head, picked up the thermos of coffee and basket of hot biscuits she'd prepared earlier and quietly closed the kitchen door.

As soon as she got to the arena, Jim opened the door. "Don't come in, Martha. You don't want you to see this."

"I understand, Jim. Just thought you might like coffee. Is there anything else I can get for you? You really need to rest; you've been up all night. Ted, too." Martha caught a glimpse of the rows of bodies covered with sheets. *My goodness, they look like ghosts waiting for Halloween. I don't want to see any more.*

"We've taken turns sleeping. We're fine." He took the tray, held it up to his face and inhaled. "Smells good. Thanks, dear. Are the children doing okay? And did the men board up the windows?"

"Yes, they did and it's considerably warmer now. We all slept downstairs. I thought we'd feel safer together. Allan kept moaning in his sleep so I moved him next to me, and Caroline cried out as if she had a terrible dream. Oh, Jim, please come home soon."

"I promise I will, dear."

"We need you."

"I know, I know. Captain Mahoney said he'd be back at eight. We'll come home then. This has been so hard for families trying to locate their loved ones and having to look at all the bodies."

"I can't imagine how horrible it must be."

"It's dreadful. You just wouldn't believe it."

"I'll expect you later, then. Oh, did you know that it's starting to snow?"

"No, just what we need, eh? We'll be home soon."

Martha glanced around the neighborhood. Except for checking on Mrs. Boudreau, it was the first time she'd seen the area since the explosion. Just as Caroline said, most houses were missing their windows. Some had completely caved in. Several porches were wrenched off by the blast, trees bent over or uprooted. Yards were strewn with broken branches, roof shingles, pieces of furniture and other debris. Martha shuddered. She wondered about her other neighbors, but felt compelled to go straight home.

She didn't want to deal with the tragedy and fled to her house, slamming the door shut. Flinging her coat and scarf onto a coat hook, Martha raced upstairs and tried to put her house back in order but a hard lump caught in her throat and tears stung her eyes.

She knelt beside a bed now devoid of a mattress and tried to pray. She couldn't. Sitting back on her heels, she silently sobbed. *Bertram, Bertie we called you. You didn't look like the others. No, your light hair was tinged with a touch of red and dimples dotted your chubby little cheeks. You sure were a charmer. Eleven months old, just starting to walk. My precious baby!*

Usually Martha appeared stoic, but today she felt especially weak and vulnerable. She supposed it was because the past year hadn't been a good one.

When she received the news that her father suffered a heart attack, Jim insisted Martha leave immediately. "I'll watch the children," he said. "We'll be fine." Martha packed a valise then rode the trolley to the dock, where she boarded the *Prince Edward Island* ferry. It was a long trip and she would have preferred to sit on the upper deck for a while, but the air was too chilly. In a way, the young woman was excited about going back. She grew up on the island and loved it there. It was an all-day trip, and being five months pregnant, she was exhausted by the time the ferry maneuvered into port. Her friend, Anna, met her and drove her directly to the hospital.

Martha ran to her mother and hugged her long and hard. "I came as soon as I could."

"I know. It's a long trip. Your father's condition is grave. Edward should be here by tonight. I'm just afraid your dad won't last that long." She dabbed at her eyes with a linen handkerchief.

Martha approached the bedside. "Hello, Father." She bent over and kissed him on the forehead. He opened his eyes in recognition of his daughter's voice but was too weak to speak. His eyes closed again. Martha took his hand although she didn't have any words for him. She felt numb and when tears threatened, stood and let her mother take her place.

Soon the doctor and a nurse came to check on his vital signs. Martha and her mother left the room. When through, the doctor approached them. He told them the prognosis was not good and he didn't expect his patient would last more than a day or two. Martha felt faint and had to sit. She didn't want to believe the doctor, although having been trained as a practical nurse she knew the signs. She didn't like what she saw. The last time they visited us he was so vibrant. *Oh, God!*

They returned to the room and sat at his bedside. Her father was asleep. Martha was the eldest in the family. Her only sibling was a younger brother, Edward, who lived in the States. As she tried to relax she thought about her life and growing up in Charlottetown on the Island.

When she awoke from her reverie, she looked at her father. His breathing was especially faint. Just then Edward tiptoed into the room and kissed both his mother and sister before kneeling beside the bed. He spoke to his father, but there was no response and soon after Richard Johns was pronounced dead.

Martha was surprised the night before the funeral when her husband arrived by late ferry. She asked. "Who's with the children?"

"Margie. She was delighted to have time with her niece and nephews. I wanted to be here for you and your mother."

"Jim, you're the kindest person I know. I love you." She hugged him close.

The day of her father's funeral was rainy and the air was raw. Jim and his brother-in-law had made arrangements with the undertaker. Mourners came to offer their condolences, congregated at St. Dunstan's Basilica for the funeral, then processed to the cemetery just one block away. When the casket was lowered into the ground the sun gloriously appeared from behind the clouds. The family took this as a good sign and returned home where neighbors had prepared sandwiches, hot tea, fresh fruit, and desserts.

Much later, when the last of the guests had departed, the family sat around the dining table and talked until very late in the evening. Ed left the following day. Martha offered to stay on, even though she knew her husband had to return to Halifax, and she was anxious to get back to her children. Her mother sensed this, so within a few days insisted her daughter take the ferry back home.

With some regrets Martha waved goodbye to her mother. The trip home was a rough one and Martha felt every jostle of the raging sea. However, when Jim met her at the dock with Ted, Caroline, and Jerry in tow, she immediately felt better. Jim had a calming effect on the whole family. The children were happy to see their mother and she was glad to be home.

Martha went into labor two months later. The midwife barely arrived when a premature baby boy was delivered. Bertram was a sickly, albeit happy child. His brothers and sister doted on him, but before he was a year old he developed meningitis and died within a few days. It was a sad time for the O'Neill family. The tiny white casket reminded Martha of a treasure box she had seen in the department store. Indeed, it did contain a treasure, her baby. Martha continued to be deeply depressed. Doctor Munroe came by daily.

"You've got to pull yourself together, Martha," he said.

"I'm trying, Doctor, but all I want to do is cry. I keep wondering if somehow he could have been saved."

"But you did everything you could. You can't continue to dwell on his death or the death of your father. You have so many good things in your life. Think of your other children. Try to think of positive things."

"I promise I'll try harder."

By Spring Martha still hadn't recovered, so Jim asked her mother to come live with them. Martha was relieved. She and her mother got along well, and her mother was a considerable help with the children, constant laundry, cooking, and she never interfered.

I guess I took the doctor's words literally, because from that day on I've hated to face any unpleasantries. It just seems easier to push them into a corner. I don't want to deal with them. What am I going to do now? I know I have to be strong for my family, even though inside I feel like I'm falling apart.

Martha heard voices. "That must be Jim and Ted." Wiping her tears, she blew her nose and straightened her apron before descending the stairs. She refilled the teakettle and set out cups and saucers. Going about her usual chores kept her from her feelings.

Chapter 8
A Long Night

Ted and his dad finally got home after the incredibly long night. And Ted didn't argue when his father suggested Ted should bathe first.

As he entered the bathroom, Ted set the kerosene lamp on a shelf on the back of the toilet, removed his clothing, and stepped into the porcelain tub. Inhaling deeply, he sank into the warm water, closed his eyes and leaned his head against the back of the tub. After the smell of the fires and the stench of sweat and debris, the scent of the Castile soap was a welcome change.

Scrubbing his hands and fingernails with a small brush, he mumbled to himself, "Ouch! More glass." Ted put his sore finger to his mouth and with his teeth pulled out the tiny splinter of glass. Bruises and scrapes had been easy to ignore in the midst of the trauma but Ted could feel them now. Picking up the washcloth, he rubbed soap over it and scrubbed the rest of his body. *I may wash away the blood but I'll never erase those images. God, I can't even talk about what I saw. I can barely believe it myself. Oh Rebecca, where are you?* The young man blinked back tears. *I know I'm lucky to be alive. It shocks me how close I came to death. Now I have to deal with reality.*

He sank even deeper in the tub, trying to block out the terrible images. He wept at remembering the tiny shoe. How he wanted to find the baby. Other scenes flashed through the young man's mind: blood spurting from Mr. Camden's neck; glass everywhere; flattened buildings; fires; bodies buried under rubble; smoke and dust. Some of the buildings—it was hard to realize a house or a store existed there just hours before. The house where Rebecca and her mother lived was missing its roof as well as the people. It was too much for him to deal with.

A knock on the bathroom door startled him. "Ted, you all right?"

"Yes, Dad, I'll be out in a minute." Ted sat up straight, then pulled the plug and watched the water as it swirled down the drain. He dried himself with the Turkish towel, then put on clean underwear, trousers, a shirt and sweater. Next, he wiped the steamy mirror with the towel and drew a comb through his dark wavy hair. He stopped and looked in the glass. He put his hand to his face. *Funny, I don't remember shaving, but I guess I did.* He splashed on a little aftershave, patting his face with his hands. It felt good. After he brushed his teeth, he picked up his soiled clothing and opened the door.

"Feel better, son?"

"Ummm, yes."

Caroline approached Ted and reached for the armload of clothes. "I'll take your things to the laundry basket."

"Now why would you want to do that?"

"Because Mama told me to. She has your breakfast ready," she said with a smirk.

The food smelled good but Ted could barely eat. He placed a forkful of scrambled eggs in his mouth but had a hard time swallowing. However, the hot coffee went down easily and felt good. Afterward he sat with his brothers and sister. "How are you guys doing?"

Jerry blurted, "Grandma held Charles because he kept crying, and they watched Mama help me down the stairs. All of a sudden the house started to shake...the windows broke. We were scared and didn't know what happened. Mrs. Boudreau broke her leg and Caroline's teacher was killed and..."

"You're telling the whole story, Jerry. Let me tell my part."

"Okay, okay. Now tell me your story, Caroline." Ted reached over, patted Jerry on the head and lifted Allan onto his lap.

"Allan and I were late for school because we were playing with Mrs. Boudreau's puppy. That reminds me, can you help me look for her tomorrow?"

Ted nodded yes, and hoped she meant the puppy and not Mrs. Boudreau.

"Sister scolded me for slamming the door but I didn't. I swear I didn't. She shoved me under her desk and a huge blast broke all the windows. Next thing we knew, we were covered with chunks of plaster and everybody was scared. I couldn't find my teacher at first, then I saw her crumpled on the floor like a rag doll and I screamed bloody blue murder." Caroline finally took a deep breath.

"What happened next?"

"The girls rushed over to me; they saw Sister and..." Big tears rolled down Caroline's cheeks.

Ted reached out to her. "It's all right, Sis. There was nothing you could do." Changing the subject he asked, "Where was Allan?"

"He was...all the boys, they were in a group, but Allan couldn't hear. He still can't. Do you think he'll ever hear again?"

"Mama told me about his not being able to hear. I'm sure he'll be fine in a couple of days. Just give it some time." He stretched and yawned. "Speaking of time, I've been up for many hours. I need sleep. You kids behave today, okay?"

He slid Allan off his lap and went up to his room. He pulled off his shoes, collapsed on the bed, and yanked a quilt up over him.

When he first put his head on the pillow his mind swarmed with the events of the previous day but exhaustion soon took over, and he fell into a troubled sleep. He kept thinking about Rebecca and her mother. *I think they'd have taken Mrs. Cranston to the hospital because she was sick, but Rebecca, what happened to her? Where is she? I'll go to the school today to be sure she's all right.*

He pictured Captain Mahoney's face when he told Ted the clock tower was destroyed. *Mr. Young and I repaired the clock on Wednesday. And now it's gone.* A scene from the past worked its way into his mind. Clocks had always held a fascination for Ted ever since he was a little kid perched on his grandfather's knee. Grandpa let me hold his pocket watch. I still remember the sound when I put it to my ear. Tick, tick, tick it went, only faster. Gold case, black hands pointing to the hour and minute. Even a sweep hand that counted the seconds. Ted recalled telling his grandfather that the watch was not ticking evenly and that he should have it repaired. The old man scoffed at the boy's concerns, but two days later the watch stopped. He had it repaired. After that he paid attention to Ted, at least about clocks and watches. Ted inherited the treasured timepiece after his grandfather died.

When the opportunity to apprentice as a watchmaker came, Ted jumped at the chance. He was a quick study and a hard worker. This pleased Mr. Young who was married but had no children. He treated Ted as if he were a son. The clocks and watches in the shop had a gentle rhythm to which Ted became attuned.

Ted continued to toss and turn. First on one side of the bed, then restlessly to the other side, not able to get comfortable, trying to keep his mind away from the dreadful scenes of the disaster. After a while he dozed again. This time he dreamed of his friend Gerald. A jumble of scenes awoke Ted. He couldn't get back to sleep so he finally got up and went downstairs.

His mother asked, "Would you like some toast?"

"No, thanks." He looked at his father. "Dad, I keep thinking about Gerald Keddy. You know he's a mechanic at the Dominion Mill. I heard the place was flattened. Do you know anything about it?"

"No, only that most everything on Barrington Street was destroyed."

"I heard that, too. Think I'll go over to see what I can find out, but first I'm going to the Chebucto School. They said many were taken there so I'm hoping Rebecca's there, too. By the way, Mother, is there anything I can do before I leave?"

"No, dear, your dad and Allan brought in wood for the stove so we're all set. It sure is snowing hard now. You be careful."

Jim set down his coffee cup. "Did you say the Chebucto School?"

"Yes. When I was in Rebecca's neighborhood they told me people were most likely taken to the school."

His father's face grew serious. "Sit down, Ted. There's something you need to know." Jim hesitated, then took a deep breath. "The school has been turned into a morgue, much like the arena with bodies awaiting identification."

"No! I thought they were taken there to be safe. I can't believe it. I won't believe it." Ted stomped over and grabbed his coat off the hook. "I'm going there today. She's alive. I know she is. She has to be, Dad." *The school, a morgue?* Not in a million years would Ted have thought that.

"I hope you're right, son. I surely do hope you are." Jim brushed a tear from his cheek.

Chapter 9
Puppy Rescue

"Ted, are you leaving?" asked Caroline.

"Yes, I am. Why?" He didn't want to talk.

"Mrs. Boudreau is still in the hospital and no one has seen her dog. I want to find it and I need your help. Mama won't let me go out alone and I'm scared the puppy may be hurt."

"I was going to check on a few things, but it is snowing hard. Guess I could help you look for the dog. It shouldn't take long. Maybe then the storm will be over." Ted stopped. *I know my sister is worried about the dog and rightly so, but it seems like I keep meeting with obstacles. I'm anxious to find Rebecca and to see if Gerald is okay.*

"I'll get my coat and mittens." When Caroline pulled her coat off the hook there was a package attached to it. "What's this? Mama, do you know what this is?"

"Grandma said it's an early Christmas present for you."

"Can I open it?"

"Ask Grandma."

Caroline found her grandmother sitting in the rocker, singing to the baby. "Grandma, is this for me? Can I open it now?"

"Of course, dear, open it."

Caroline quickly tore the colorful paper off the package, revealing a long scarf of many colors. "Oh, Grandma, it's beautiful. Thank you." She hugged her grandmother and planted a kiss on her cheek.

"I know you lost your hat. I made this scarf for you for Christmas, but it's as good a time as any to give it to you. Merry Christmas, dear."

"I love it. It reminds me of Joseph's coat in the Bible. Thank you, Grandma," said the happy girl, wrapping it over her head and around her neck. "It's perfect." This time she blew a kiss as she left.

"Let's go," said Ted.

"I'm ready."

They opened the kitchen door and a swirl of white came sailing in. "Close the door quickly," scolded Mama.

The snow hadn't accumulated much but the swirling around made it difficult to see. The two went straight to the Boudreau house. Caroline had noticed the pile of rubble on her way home from school. The porch had been torn away, exposing part of the cellar, and the rest of the structure had caved in. A fire still smoldered under the beams. She was shocked. *Oh my, what if the dog is dead?*

"Here, Pumpkin. Here, puppy," Caroline called.

Ted whistled for the dog to no avail.

"Wait, Ted, I think I heard something."

"It's just the wind." He whistled again.

"Shhh, listen," said Caroline, pulling her scarf away from her ears. "Did you hear that? I think it came from down there." She pointed in the direction of the cellar.

Ted wasn't sure he heard anything that sounded like a puppy barking or even whimpering but placated his sister by following her. He stopped. "I did hear it, Sis. Sounds like it's down there. Wait right here." He climbed over broken glass and other rubble, moving a broken chair from his path.

"Come here, Pumpkin, it's okay," called Caroline. She stayed back while her brother looked for the dog.

"I'm sure she's down there, but I can't get into the cellar. Come over here, Sis, maybe you can fit down the hole."

Caroline moved closer to her brother. She looked at the narrow opening.

"I don't know if I can get in that small space either. Oh, it's so dark down there. Here, puppy, come on." Caroline was bundled against the cold and snow and was too bulky to fit into the tight space. She removed her heavy coat and multi-colored scarf.

"You'll freeze to death," admonished her brother. *Maybe we should find another way into the cellar*, he thought. *What if it isn't safe? I'd never forgive myself if Caroline got hurt.* "Wait. Don't go in there, it could be dangerous. We'll find another way."

"No, I won't freeze. It's just until I can get the puppy. I'll be all right. I just hope I can get to her in time. I don't want her to freeze to death either." The girl squiggled into the dark space of the cellar. It was eerie. She always hated the dark to begin with but was intent on finding her neighbor's puppy. *It's so cute and friendly*, she thought. *I just have to find it.* She tripped over the leg of an overturned table but caught her balance and cautiously peered around a corner. "I think I found her. She's here. Oh, she's shaking. Ted, toss down my scarf. I'll wrap her in it."

Ted dropped the scarf to his sister. "Be careful, Caroline. Just wrap up the puppy. I'll reach for it."

Caroline picked up the shivering animal and cuddled it to her chest, like her mother might do. The puppy licked her face. "Oh, you poor darling, you must be scared. Everything will be okay now. Here, Ted, can you reach her?"

Ted got down on his stomach and extended his arms into the hole. He grabbed the little bundle and set it on the ground, then helped his sister up.

Once Caroline was out of the cellar she bent over the pitiful puppy and scooped it up in her arms. Ted took the pup back from Caroline while she put her coat on. She wrapped the scarf around the dog and hurried home. It was blustery and they were chilled to the bone.

"What's this?" asked Martha. "Why aren't you wearing your scarf, Caroline?"

"Mama, look, it's Mrs. Boudreau's puppy. Her name is Pumpkin."

"I'm glad you found her and I surely can see why she's named that. Why she's exactly the color of a pumpkin, isn't she?"

"Can we keep her here, just until Mrs. Boudreau comes home?"

"I don't know, dear, we'll have to ask your father later. He's resting now. We'll feed her and perhaps she'll feel better. Let me get a towel so you can dry her off."

The puppy shivered. When Caroline put it on the floor, it whimpered as it tried to walk. Ted picked her up and examined her paws. "I think her feet were burned or something. Mama, can you take a look?"

Martha came back with a towel. "Let me see," she said taking the puppy from her son. Sitting in a chair and placing the animal on her lap, she said. "Hi, little pup; let's see what's wrong." Her paws were in bad shape, most likely from frostbite or being burned from the fires.

"Ted, go to the medicine cabinet and get me the ointment in the beige tube. Caroline, fetch two pairs of the baby's white socks from the clean laundry basket." Martha stroked the dog's head. It trembled.

"Here you go," said Ted handing the ointment to his mother.

Caroline gave her the socks and bent over the injured animal. "Poor little pumpkin puppy. My Mama will take good care of you, little sweetheart." The puppy responded by licking Caroline's hand while Martha applied the ointment. Martha then fashioned the socks into little booties for the puppy.

"I'll need to tie them on with something. Get me a spool of thread, dear."

"Sure." Caroline got a spool of thread from the sewing table. "Can I help?"

"Yes, keep the puppy occupied while I tie these on her. She keeps biting at them. She thinks they're a toy and will probably try tear them off, but if we can keep them on awhile, I'm sure her feet will feel better," said Martha as she secured the little socks.

"She's not shivering now and looks so cute in her little booties. Maybe Mrs. Boudreau will have to change her name to *Boots*."

"Let's get some nourishment into the little mutt. She must be hungry after all this time." Martha handed the dog back to Caroline and went to the pantry. Soon she was back with a couple of crackers which she crushed into a small bowl, then added an egg and finally mixed in a little of the chopped meat they were having for dinner that night. She threw in a few green peas for good measure. When it was well mixed she said, "Keep her in your lap, Caroline. If she gets down she'll surely pull off the bandages."

Caroline took the dish from her mother and held it close to the puppy. It ate ravenously. When the dish was empty, Ted brought over a small bowl of water. The pup quickly licked it dry. Then Caroline let her patient sleep in her lap, although it wasn't for long because soon Gerald hobbled into the kitchen with Allan by his side. They were excited when they saw the puppy and couldn't wait to play with it.

Bundled up again, Ted attempted to go to the Chebucto School, but the fierce wind and blinding snow forced him to turn back after a few blocks. The wind practically blew him home. Feeling defeated, he walked up the steps and into the house, hung up his coat and sat at the kitchen table. The house felt warm and safe.

"I'm having a cup of tea. Can I make you some?" asked Grandma.

"No thanks."

Grandma set her cup next to her grandson. "I'm sorry the storm is keeping you from finding your friends, Ted. When it's over you can go out again. For now, perhaps you need to rest."

"On second thought, I'd love a cup of tea." He reached over and covered the woman's hand with his.

Grandma smiled, patted his hand, then got another cup. She added tea to the infuser and set it into the cup before pouring in boiling water from the kettle.

Ted wrapped his hands around the cup while the tea steeped. The warmth felt good. "Thanks, but I'm not sleepy. I am exhausted but part of it's from worry. Grandma, if you'd seen Rebecca's house you'd be worried too. I just hope they were able to get out in time." *I need to find her. I need to find a way.*

Chapter 10
Putting the Pieces Together

The storm, which began as a gentle flurry, increased. A fierce wind reduced visibility as the snow swirled and drifted. People remained indoors if they had a place to stay. Lack of windows and doors made it difficult to keep warm.

Just when people thought things couldn't get any worse, they did. As the raging blizzard on Friday subsided, the weather turned balmy but was followed by torrential rains. Soon streets, looking more like rivers than roads, were knee-deep in slush. People used doors, boards, and boxes to prevent snow and slush from coming indoors. By late afternoon the tempest stopped and the wind died down.

"At last, a break," said Jim with a sigh. However, within a few hours conditions changed once again and temperatures dropped rapidly. The weather, echoing the events, was erratic.

"I'm happy the children found the puppy before all this snow and ice came, and I'm very glad Ted decided to wait for the storm to cease, but tell me, Jim, I still am not sure. What did happen? I mean do they know what caused the explosion?" asked Martha.

Jim paused, staring into space before he answered. "From what I can gather, two ships collided in the harbor. The munitions ship was laden with picric acid and TNT. Some say it held over two tons of explosives. The collision started a fire, igniting the volatile chemicals. Although the crew tried to put it out, it was hopeless and they were ordered to abandon ship. Most of them got into lifeboats and rowed to the Dartmouth side. At least that's what I heard."

"Thank the good Lord for that. How fortunate we are." Martha refilled her husband's coffee cup.

Jim took a sip of the hot liquid. "You're right, dear. Even so, there isn't much we can do, especially with the weather. I feel helpless. I want to check on Carl and his family. We haven't heard a word from them."

"I agree you should see your brother, Jim. But please wait for a break in the storm." Martha stood and smoothed her apron. "I feel blessed now that our house is secure and we're all together. I want to see how our neighbors have fared. Perhaps I'll go out tomorrow."

Martha had no way of knowing that when the storm was over everything would freeze solid. In a way it was a good thing because it would be weeks before bodies could be buried. If the weather had been warmer, the deteriorating corpses would have forced authorities to bury them in mass graves rather than waiting for them to be identified.

The wind and cold penetrated the walls of the O'Neill house, even though the furnace was stoked with coal and the kitchen stove was filled with wood. The children wore extra sweaters and wrapped quilts around themselves.

"Let me change those bandages," suggested Martha.

"I'll be fine," replied Jim. "You've already got your hands full."

"But I need to check those deep gashes, the ones covered with the lint."

"If you insist. You're the nurse." Jim smiled lovingly at his wife as he sat in the designated chair. Martha carefully and methodically removed each bandage. Some cuts were healing nicely, but others were red and angry from the onslaught of infection. Martha daubed the cuts with iodine.

"How does your eye feel, dear?"

"It still feels scratchy but it's surely better than before. My arm's better too; must have just wrenched it. My only complaint now is this headache. I can't seem to get rid of it."

"It might take time, but if you still have it after the weekend, try to see Doctor Munroe. Take Allan with you. Maybe he'll see you both."

"That's a good idea. Meanwhile, do you have anything I can take?"

"Yes, I'll get some aspirin."

While his wife went for the medicine, Jim fought the feeling of something being terribly wrong. *I can't see out of my right eye now, and the headache never subsides. Aspirin takes the pain down but not for long. Guess I'll have to see Doc Munroe after all.*

Unaware that her husband was blind in his right eye, Martha thought his headaches were temporary. She was also unaware of the dreadful devastation that had taken place outside and assumed life would go on as usual.

Jim didn't want to worry her, so for the rest of the day he, Martha and Ted worked at putting the upstairs back together. They swept and dusted, then carried the mattresses back upstairs and made the beds once again. Except for the windows, which were hastily boarded up, the second floor looked normal.

Meanwhile downstairs, Caroline read to the younger boys, keeping her voice loud for Allan whose hearing improved a little each day. After awhile they played, *I'm thinking of a color.* So that Allan could participate easily, they first pointed to a color so the guessers would know what to look for. That worked out well and Allan quickly adapted.

Grandma cooked supper and afterward spread a jigsaw puzzle out on a card table in a corner of the parlor. Jerry and Allan put a few pieces together. Soon the outer edges were nearly complete. Working on the puzzle took their minds off the tragedy and before long they laughed and joked the way they always had.

"Oh, Grandma, I almost forgot," said Caroline. "Yesterday was supposed to be the Art Fair. They were going to judge our projects. I was hoping to win again this year. Now I wonder if there is anything left."

"I know you're disappointed, my dear, but there are much more important things to tend to right now. If your painting was destroyed, you can paint another. The next one might be even better."

"I guess you're right, Grandma, I'm being selfish."

"No, not selfish, Caroline, you're being a thirteen-year-old." She smiled and gave the girl a hug. "Come help us with the puzzle."

Later, the rest of the family joined them in the parlor.

"Ted, why don't you play us a tune? Maybe it will keep you from pacing the floor;" his father suggested.

The upright piano stood against a wall in the parlor. Ted raised the cover exposing the keys, took music from the bench and began to play. *I don't feel like playing but they enjoy it and let's face it, I'm not much good to anyone if I continue to mope.* As his nimble fingers ran over the keys, the family visibly relaxed. Ted played Beethoven's "Für Elise," a favorite of Martha's. Next he played a Sonatina, then a minuet by Mozart.

Looking up from the music, he said, "I've been practicing, 'Clair de Lune.' I'll play a little of it." The music was soothing and even Jim's headache seemed to lessen. Although Ted usually enjoyed playing the piano for his family, tonight he played without feeling. He still was numb with anguish and worry.

The family retired early that night, sleeping in their own rooms. Ted lay awake for most of the night, thinking about Rebecca and Gerald. He prayed unceasingly for their safekeeping.

On Sunday the roads were solid ice, so the family decided not to risk going to Mass. Instead, they gathered around the kitchen table, taking turns reading from the Bible and reciting the rosary together. When they were through, Martha made pancakes with maple syrup and bacon as a treat for everyone. For the remainder of the day they worked on the puzzle and talked about the explosion and how they would rebuild their lives. Ted and Caroline played duets on the piano and Ted played songs they could sing to. It was a momentary healing time for the family.

Chapter 11
My Buddy

By Monday the weather changed once more, only this time for the better. It didn't feel as cold. It was a gradual thaw so that streets and sidewalks, what remained of them, could be cleared of ice, snow, and debris.

Ted went to the jewelry shop, hoping the place hadn't been looted. He felt responsible, being in charge on that dreadful day. Fear gripped him when he found the shop unlocked but was relieved when Mr. Young came to the door.

"Ted, thank God you're all right." Mr. Young reached to shake hands with his apprentice, changed his mind and pulled Ted to his chest in a hug. "We heard about the explosion but couldn't get back, what with the weather and all. When I saw all the blood I feared the worst. Tell me what happened."

Ted described how Mr. Camden had come in for his wristwatch, how the blast shook the store and knocked Ted off his feet. He told him about the overturned case, and how he tried to save Mr. Camden to no avail. Ted's hands shook.

Mr. Young said softly, "It's okay, son. Just take your time. I'm sure you did the best you could."

"Blood was spurting from his neck. I couldn't stop it. I couldn't save him." Tears flowed down Ted's cheeks. Embarrassed, he blew his nose before continuing. He told Mr. Young how the Rescue Squad came for the body.

"Captain Mahoney warned me about looters."

"I'm just glad you're okay. At first I thought it was you who was killed. Your family, they're all right are they?"

"Yes, we were lucky. The arena roof collapsed on Dad. Henry dug him out. My father had over fifty cuts but he's alive and for that we're grateful."

"I guess so. Hope your dad will be okay. I'm sorry you had to witness Basil Camden's gory death. I know it must have been just horrible. I'm sorry I wasn't here to shield you from that."

"It was pretty gruesome, and it's hard to describe the feeling of dread we all had."

"I'm sure. Now what brings you here today? I doubt we'll have any customers."

For the first time, a smile appeared on Ted's face. "I know. I just stopped to see if the place was okay. I'm going to the Chebucto School to find Rebecca and her mother, then to see if Gerald is okay. By the way, was anything stolen?"

"No, I don't think so. I had help getting the display case back up. A number of items were broken but for the most part everything is here. I noticed that you put many things into the locked cabinet in back. Good thinking."

"I'm glad. See you later." Ted opened the door to leave.

"Things will be fine here. I have a few things to do right now, Ted. If you check on Gerald first, I'll drive you to the school when you get back. It's quite a hike from here."

"No, I want to check on Rebecca." He hesitated. "But it does make sense to go to the mill first. I'll see about Gerald, then stop back."

Ted was relieved now that Mr. Young was home. He shuddered when he saw the piles of smoldering rubble as he headed for Barrington Street. The mill was decimated. No one could tell him if there were survivors. Ted was visibly upset. *What if Gerald is dead? And his sister? She worked there, too.* From the appearance of the area Ted couldn't imagine how anyone could have survived. *I'd better see his family, if nothing else than to offer my condolences. God, I hope he missed work that day.* Ted knew it was unlikely for Gerald to miss work.

The Dartmouth Ferry was operating and Ted didn't have to wait long before the blast of the horn signaled it was ready to embark.

He sat, looking out over the water. The salty air was a nice change from the acrid odor of the fires. He felt sad and wondered how Gerald's family would take the bad news. Ted and Gerald had been best friends for a long time. They met one summer when they were both ten years old and had been best buddies ever since.

Ted remembered how Gerald helped him when he and his father built their summer house on the top of a hill, overlooking the cove. *Dad called us his gophers. Go for this, go for that. Hand me my saw, get that piece of lumber. Very inventive, my dad once forgot his plumb line, or rather I neglected to return it to his toolbox. He found a small bottle, rigged a string around the neck, filled it half full of water and voila, a plumb line. It worked. With the help of some of Dad's friends it didn't take long before we were staying there for the summer. We all loved it. Mother named it Summerhill, which was appropriate. The cottage was large and consisted of many rooms. We all agreed that the porch was the best as it wrapped around the entire downstairs. On hot summer nights the family slept there; that is, if the mosquitoes didn't chase us away. During the day there was always a breeze and the view was outstanding.*

A toddler crawled up on the bench beside Ted, diverting his attention for the moment. He moved to make room for the child's mother. Gazing over the water and watching the wake, Ted's thoughts kept returning to Rebecca. *No, I can't think about her now, I'm too emotional. I'm afraid she's hurt and I feel guilty I couldn't find her that first day. But right now I've got to see Gerald's family. I have to think of more pleasant times.*

Smiling, Ted recalled the birthday present he got for Gerald when he turned fourteen. Ted had a friend whose uncle worked for the Canadian Explosions Company and he gave Ted a pile of shotgun shells. Ted put them in a small wooden box, then inside a larger box and again in yet an even bigger box. He nailed each one shut. Ted and Allan took the package to Gerald who was stacking bales of hay in the loft. The day was hot, the smell of the hay pleasant.

"Here you go," said Ted, handing Gerald a box.

"What's this?" queried his friend.

"It's your birthday present." Allan looked smug.

Gerald climbed down from the loft. He tried to open the box, shook his head, found a small pinch bar in the tool shed and pried the nails from the cover. He laughed when he saw another box inside. "Hey, what kind of sick joke is this?"

"We just wanted to protect your present," said Ted.

When all the boxes were opened, there sat the pile of shells. "Wow!" Gerald scratched his head. "What are we gonna use 'em for? Target practice?"

"Sure, we could target practice with them but I have a better idea." Ted whispered something to his friend.

"No way! You kiddin'?"

"Listen. Who do you know who's up at midnight? No harm will come, you'll see."

"Okay, first help me with the hay."

Ted tossed bales of hay to Gerald, who stacked them in the loft. When they were finished, Ted grabbed little Allan by the seat of his pants and tossed him up to Gerald. "Here's the last one. Catch!"

"Wow, I'm flying!" the little boy squealed.

"He likes it. I'm sending him back to you." Just then the seat of Allan's pants let go with a big rip.

Allan pouted and a tear spilled down his cheek. "Mama's gonna be mad."

"There, there. We'll fix you up," said Ted as he went to the tack shop. He found a large needle and heavy thread used to repair leather harnesses. The fact that Allan's britches were light blue didn't faze

Ted as he threaded the needle with the black thread and sewed his brother's pants. "Just like new."

"What are we going to tell Mama?"

"The truth. I'll tell her I grabbed you when you nearly fell from the loft and your pants ripped. She'll be happy I saved you. Come on, little buddy. Bye Gerald, see you tonight. Don't forget; have the horses ready."

Just before midnight Ted slipped from his bed and quietly left the house. He trotted the half mile to his friend's house. Gerald was waiting by the gate with the horses and two shotguns.

Later, Caroline told him she was dreaming about the fireworks they'd seen earlier. It frightened her and she jumped out of bed, grabbed her dressing gown and headed for her parent's bedroom. Her Dad was pulling his suspenders up over his shoulder with one hand while the other held a pistol.

"I screamed. 'Daddy! What is it?' He told me to stay there and dashed out of the house. "At first I thought we were being attacked and ran to Mama. Mama told me I could get into their big bed. She checked the boy's room. They were all sleeping, except for you. You weren't there. Mama checked the porch and you were not there, either. She said she couldn't recall if you went out with Daddy or not. So together we prayed that all would be well. We sure were nervous. It was a long time before Daddy returned. By then we were up and had a pot of coffee brewing."

"What is it, Jim?" Martha questioned.

"I'm not sure. They say a gang came through town on horses, yelling and shooting up the place, making all kinds of noise. They didn't hit anything. I think they just wanted to scare us."

"Do they know who it was?"

"No, but I have a feeling." He looked around. "Where's Ted?"

"I don't know, dear, I thought he was with you."

"You mean he isn't home?"

Caroline suddenly remembered Allan saying something about a box of ammunition they got for Gerald. But she pursed her lips and didn't say a word.

"I didn't want to get you in trouble," Caroline told Ted.

"Well, I got in plenty of trouble. We just wanted to have a little fun. We weren't out to hurt anyone. Do you remember how much wood I chopped and stacked for the next few weeks? That was my punishment. Why, we had enough wood for a blizzard, not that we needed it in the summer."

The ferry continued to chug across Bedford Basin. The blast of the horn brought Ted back to reality. They were nearing Dartmouth. As they came through the end of the harbor and into the narrows, Ted could see Glassy Island. The Keddy farm was located just up the hill, barn on the right, then the house.

Ted stood, straightened his jacket, and adjusted his cap in anticipation for the ferry to come to a halt. He walked down the ramp and headed for the farm. As he trudged through the little village and up the familiar path, he became more apprehensive. There didn't appear to be any damage from the explosion on the hill. Everything looked the same as always. *If only that were true. What if? What if?*

Ted kicked a stone from the pathway as he neared the house and hesitated before cautiously knocking on the kitchen door. He looked down. His hands were shaking. A cold sweat ran down his neck and he wanted to run away. Instead, he took a deep breath. Someone was coming to the door. The door swung open. Ted was astonished and delighted. It was Gerald.

Opening his mouth to say hello, Ted then grabbed his friend in a bear hug as tears welled in his eyes. "Hey, you old dog, you made it out."

Gerald hugged him back. "And you? You look none the worse for the wear."

"I think I'm the luckiest guy in Halifax, next to you." Ted wiped his sweaty brow with his handkerchief. "Man, I really thought you were dead."

"My sister didn't make it."

"Oh, no!"

"It was terrible. Most were killed in the factory. Only a few survived. I searched and searched for my sister but couldn't find her. Last night my parents were informed that the bodies of several girls were found. Dad identified Mary."

"I'm so sorry. What an awful thing to happen to such a beautiful person. Oh, that's the worst!" Ted shouldn't have been surprised. He saw the mill and really didn't expect that anyone survived. "Aw, Gerald, can I see your Mom and Dad; tell them how sorry I am?"

Ted followed Gerald into the kitchen. His parents sat at the oilcloth-covered table. It was obvious Mrs. Keddy had been crying. She got up when Ted came in, wrapped her arms around him and burst into sobs. Ted hugged her and told them both how sorry he was. It was awkward because there was always so much laughter in the Keddy household.

They offered him cake and coffee. He stayed for a little while although he didn't have any words to say. What could he say to a family who had just lost its only daughter?

He left with a promise to return soon and hopped the ferry back to Halifax. He had expected to express his condolences to the Keddys for the loss of Gerald, but his best friend was saved. He knew the family could rejoice in that. Yet, Gerald's sister was killed. It just didn't make sense.

Chapter 12
Rebecca

This time, instead of sitting on a bench on the ferry, Ted stood watching without really seeing the wake or other people on the boat. *Rebecca. Is it possible she was lucky too? I love her so. Wonder why I never got up the courage to tell her? Please be safe, my love.* Ted blew a kiss into the wind.

Soon the ferry pulled into Halifax Harbor. The strong wind pierced Ted's coat. He adjusted the collar, pulled down his hat, and plodded past the desolation and up the hill to the jewelry repair shop.

"Ted, I was beginning to worry," said Mr. Young. "Did you find Gerald? Is he okay?"

"Yes, he is. However, his sister was killed in the blast and their parents are beside themselves with anguish. I didn't know what to say to them."

"I'm really sorry. My wife and I will call on them tomorrow." Mr. Young grabbed his hat and coat. "Come on, I'll drive you to the school."

On the way they remarked on the damage, talked about the cause of the blast and what a task it would be to rebuild. Before long they were at the school. Ted wasn't sure just what to expect. He hoped that not everyone who was taken there was dead, that maybe some were injured while others were helping them. He hesitated then said, "I don't know if I can do it."

Mr. Young turned off the engine. "I'll go in with you, Ted. You need to find out one way or the other."

Ted straightened up. "That's okay. I'll go by myself. And I can walk home from here. Thanks for the ride."

"Are you sure?" Mr. Young asked. He sensed that Ted would need time by himself.

Ted nodded, closed the car door and walked away. He drew in a deep breath and opened the door to the school. Bodies lay in lines along the hallway, much like they were in the arena. Ted's head reeled with the odor of charred and decaying flesh. He grabbed hold of a chair near the desk.

An older man asked, "Can I help you?"

"My girlfriend and her mother...their house collapsed and the work crew said they might be here."

"What's the name?" the man asked picking up his clipboard.

"Cranston."

"Let's see...Cranston. First names?"

"Rebecca, and I think her mother's name is Harriet."

The man traced the list with his index finger. "Here they are. Did you say you were a relative?"

"No, a friend. They have no relatives here. Mrs. Cranston has family in Moncton."

"Do you know their names and address so we can notify them?"

"Yes, Sullivan. John and Josephine Sullivan and they have a daughter, Cheryl. I don't know the street, only that they live in Moncton."

"Thanks, that's helpful."

"Excuse me please. Are the Cranstons alive?"

"Forgive me. I've been working too many hours. First we had to repair windows and structural damage before a steady procession of wagons and sleighs delivered the bodies. Soldiers were on hand to identify victims whenever possible and attached numbered tickets with the available information before covering them with sheets."

He looked at his clipboard again. "Harriet Cranston was dead on arrival and her daughter was taken to Mount Olivet Hospital. Do you think you can you identify the woman for me?"

Ted backed away. "I'd rather not but I can describe Mrs. Cranston. She was quite thin, sick with tuberculosis. She had dark hair with streaks of grey."

"Thank you."

Ted couldn't wait to get out. He said goodbye to the man and quickly departed. He practically danced his way to the hospital, slipping and sliding over icy patches. "She's alive! She's alive! Thank you, Lord."

Daylight was fading rapidly by the time Ted got to the hospital which appeared to have endured only minor damage. The interior of the hospital was a beehive of activity. Doctors, nurses, firemen, and volunteers all hustled about, some pushing litters or wheelchairs, others simply comforting those in pain either from their injuries or the trauma of losing loved ones.

Ted approached the reception desk. "I'm looking for Rebecca Cranston," he said to the volunteer on duty. She searched a long roster before she finally found the name.

"Are you a relative?"

"No, ma'am, I'm not. Her mother was killed and she doesn't have any other relatives here. Rebecca is my girlfriend."

"The girl is in the intensive care unit so you will have to talk with the nurse at that station. It's on the second floor." She pointed to the stairwell.

Ted took the stairs two at a time. He was anxious to see his sweetheart. When he got to the intensive care unit he hesitated until a nurse asked if she could help.

"I'm looking for my girlfriend, Rebecca Cranston. I was told I could find her here."

"I'm sorry," said the nurse, "only immediate families are allowed to see patients on this floor." She turned to walk away.

"But you don't understand," said Ted, swallowing the lump that was rapidly forming in his throat. "There is no family. Her mother was killed. I must see her. Please, I must."

"She's unconscious."

"I didn't know that." Ted paused. "Do you think I could see her anyway?"

"I shouldn't. However, under the circumstances…follow me." She led the way down a long corridor.

"Even though she's in a coma, I think it's important that you speak to her as she may very well hear you. Please," she cautioned, "don't tell her that her mother is dead. She doesn't need to know that just yet. Speak to her as you ordinarily would."

"I understand."

The nurse opened the door to Rebecca's room. At first Ted thought he was in the wrong room because the person in the bed didn't look at all like Rebecca. This person's face was swollen and bandaged. He turned to leave, then noticed the silky black of Rebecca's hair. His heart was in his throat as he approached the bed.

The nurse spoke first. "Rebecca, you have a visitor."

Ted swallowed. "Rebecca, it's me, Ted." He wanted to cry when he saw her bruised and almost unrecognizable face. Her eyes were closed and the top of her head was bandaged. Her left arm was wrapped in gauze. As Ted moved closer to her bedside, he spoke again. "Rebecca, can you hear me?"

Although she didn't open her eyes, the girl stirred.

"I saw your mother." He couldn't and wouldn't tell her that her mother was dead, but he knew she would be most concerned about her. Then he told her that his family was okay, what they thought happened, and how there were many buildings destroyed. "I'm glad you're alive. I was so worried. Can you open your eyes? Can you hear me?" He picked up her hand and it opened as if to invite Ted to hold it. He bent over, put his lips to her fingers and said, "Rebecca, I love you."

A shudder went through the injured girl. The nurse, who was standing by saw this. She grabbed her stethoscope and put it to Rebecca's heart. She listened for a long while, noted the time on her watch. She shook her head.

Ted could feel Rebecca's soft hand become limp and he knew.

Yes, he knew. He didn't want to believe it, even though it was true. His precious love had left him; gone in that instant.

The doctor entered the room, looked into the patient's eyes and checked for a pulse. He shook his head and murmured, "I'm so sorry."

Chapter 13
Too Much Sorrow

"Never hurt a soul. Why did she have to die? Why?" Ted asked, trance like, as he trudged home that night. "It just can't be." He kicked at a pile of rubble on the side of the road then screamed every curse word he knew. "She didn't deserve to die. She was such a good person."

Jim O'Neill, sitting at the kitchen table when Ted came in, didn't have to ask, he knew by looking at his son the news was not good. Jim approached him with open arms. Ted sobbed against his father's chest, then wiped his eyes and sat at the table. Jim went to the pantry, opened a cabinet and pulled out the whiskey bottle then took down two small glasses from the shelf, filling them. "Here, son, drink this."

Ted was surprised but too distraught to say anything. He looked at the glass on the table. He'd heard of people drowning their sorrows in booze. He never drank alcohol, though Gerald and he shared a beer once. They didn't like the taste and thought it smelled like skunk. "How can anyone drink this crap?" they'd remarked, but drank it anyway. *Does it work?* he wondered as he slowly picked up the glass. He smelled the dark liquid first before taking a sip. "Ugh," he shuddered.

"No, son, gulp it down all at once," his father said softly. "Like this." Jim drank the whiskey.

"Really? You sure?" Ted picked up the glass again and this time did what his father did. His eyes watered and the liquid burned all the way down his throat into his stomach. Shortly after it seemed to soothe his nerves.

"Want to talk about it?" his father asked.

"Rebecca. She's dead. Her mother's dead, too."

"They were lovely people, Rebecca and her mother. Oh, Ted, I'm so sorry. Mrs. Cranston was gravely ill so we have to believe she suffers no longer."

Ted nodded. "But what about Rebecca? She wasn't sick."

"That's a tough one. I don't have an answer. All I can say is that she'll never ever be sick or have a pain or suffer a loss. And you know she has to be in Heaven."

"And what about the rest of us? What about me? I loved Rebecca. I know Mother and Grandma and the kids loved her. You did, too. What about us? Why do we have to suffer?" Ted got up and paced the floor.

"Sorry, son, I just don't know."

Ted sat back down and reached his hand out. "I know, Dad. It's okay. You're suffering too, and here I am keeping you up all night." Ted was aware his father had endured injuries of his own and continued with constant headaches.

"Let's get to bed. In the morning we can see if Uncle Carl is all right. Okay?"

"Thanks. You sure are a comfort to your father and here I had hoped to comfort you."

"Dad, you always do. You seem to have the right words every time. This is difficult now, but I know I'm not the only one suffering. Poor Mrs. Camden, no husband and those little kids with no father. They must be frightened."

His father rose. "Yes, let's get to bed. We have a long hike tomorrow."

On Tuesday Ted and his father walked the three miles to Richmond in search of Carl and his family. The ice had thawed so it was spongy under foot. They trudged through the streets, bypassing heaps of ash and rubble, extremely aware of how few people were around the usually busy section of town. For a long while they didn't see anyone. It was eerily quiet. The area looked like a war zone, devastated.

Jim's jaw tightened. He clenched his teeth and fists. His whole body became rigid, steeling for what he feared was to come. "Good Lord, I hope it's not this way at Carl's."

They passed St. Joseph's elementary school, a pile of bricks and broken desks. "I can't believe it," he said. "The school is nothing but dust. Where are the children and the teachers?" The cornerstone with the date inscribed was all that was left, a reminder of what once was. Next door, the drug store stood intact. Jim pointed. "How do you figure it?"

"That's incredible!" Ted exclaimed, feeling a little hopeful. "Maybe Uncle Carl was lucky, too." The candy store was shattered and more houses and shops flattened than left standing. "There are many more buildings destroyed here than I thought there'd be. Reminds me of pictures I've seen of wartime France."

Ted noticed the glassiness in his father's eyes as they approached Summer Street. "It's terrible, Dad. It's even worse than the West Side where I was Thursday. But…look over there!" Ted pointed and they both breathed a sigh of relief when they saw one, two, then three homes standing. The sigh was short-lived, however because when they got to Carl's house there was nothing there but smoke curling up from the ruins. Everything was tinged a shade of grey.

"Oh, God, no!" Jim sobbed.

"But Dad, we don't know if they got out. Let's ask those workmen." Ted pointed toward the workers. He had never seen his father cry, not even when his own parents died. Ted's heart ached for him. He could only imagine how his dad must feel.

Six workmen, all with shovels, were digging inch by inch through the wet ash and dumping it into wheelbarrows.

"Do you know about the people?" asked Jim.

"Nope. Don't know. Maybe Vinnie knows. Hey, Vinnie."

The man named Vinnie looked up. "I'm not sure; think they're all dead."

Ted shouted and pointed to where his uncle's house once stood. "What about the people in this house?"

"I don't know." He scooped another shovel of ash into the wheelbarrow.

"Where'd they take the bodies, do you know?" asked Jim, trying to take a deep breath as he clutched his chest.

"Saint Mary's or the morgue."

When he heard that, Jim took a step backward to keep from collapsing.

Ted grabbed his father's arm to steady him. "Let's go to the hospital first, Dad. Maybe they were injured. Come on."

They didn't talk as they walked, each trapped in his own thoughts. Ted reflected on his cousins, John and Kenneth. They were the same age as his brothers, Jerry and Allan. He wondered about Uncle Carl and Aunt Liz and the new baby. *It was a girl but I haven't seen her. From the looks of their house, I don't see how they could have survived. And all this time we thought we'd been spared a family loss.* He shook his head to clear his thoughts. *I can't think this way. I know some survived, even when it seemed impossible for them to.*

Ted thought about how he helped to bring bodies out from the rubble when suddenly, they'd find a person alive. It just didn't make sense who was dead and who survived. "Like, why Rebecca?" The dead lined the sidewalk, the same as all those bodies in the arena or the school. How sad it was when their loved ones came. Many badly injured and in shock themselves, hoping against hope that their loved ones weren't among those shrouded on the sidewalk. It was hard to make sense of it. Ted put his hand on his dad's shoulder to confirm they were both survivors.

Saint Mary's Hospital was seven blocks uphill. Jim's head was pounding by the time they neared the facility. Breathless, he panted, "I've got to stop for a moment." He sat on the granite steps that led to a no longer-existing building.

"Are you all right?" Ted was concerned. It wasn't like his father to be weak. He had always been the strong one in the family.

"I will be shortly. I just need to catch my breath. Between seeing my brother's house and this blasted headache, well, it just got to me."

A few minutes later, Jim stood. Ted put his arm through his father's and they walked into the hospital. The smell of antiseptic and another scent Ted couldn't identify was overwhelming. *I just hope I can keep it together*. They approached the reception desk and inquired about Carl, his wife, and the children.

The receptionist pulled out a clipboard and went down the list, name after name after name. To Ted it seemed they had been standing there forever before she spoke. "Just a moment. Please wait." She got up and rapped lightly on a door behind her.

A woman dressed in white soon appeared, nodded when the receptionist spoke, then came over to the men. "Hello, I'm Myrtle Jones." She shook hands with Jim and Ted. "How can I help?" She looked crisp, yet there was a warmth about her.

Jim told her about his brother's family and where they lived.

"So many were killed." She looked at her list. "I'm so sorry to tell you this, but it shows they recovered the bodies of Carl O'Neill, a woman who presumably was his wife, and a boy."

Jim's face turned gray. Ted again put his arm around his father to steady him. Both looked down at the floor, searching for an answer or at least a reason for this nightmare.

70

Chapter 14
A Tiny Miracle

"Sometimes when everything seems the darkest there's a bright spot, a rainbow. There was a survivor taken from that house. Was there a baby in the family?" asked the nurse.

Jim's face brightened and a gleam of hope entered his voice. "Yes. They have a daughter about three months old."

"Well, it appears this child is just about that age and is a female."

"Must be little Mary Elizabeth. Is she all right?"

"Yes. She seems fine. I'll take you to the nursery."

Jim put his hand up. "But wait. They have a second son, a six-year-old."

Miss Jones looked at the roster again. "No, they only listed a man, estimated age early thirties, a woman late twenties, and one boy, probably about nine years old."

"Dad, do you suppose Kenneth was at school?" When they walked by the pile of bricks that was once St. Joseph's School, Ted wondered if his cousin went there. And now he knew. Most likely Kenneth was there. "Were there any survivors at the elementary school?"

"I'm not sure," Miss Jones said sympathetically. "We don't have those lists yet."

"Can you tell me where they took the bodies?"

"Of course." She fingered down the list. "They were taken to the Chebucto School. You could inquire there. Go and check on them."

"I was just there," said Ted. If only he had known. He could have identified his uncle, aunt, and cousins. *Poor Dad, now he has to go through that agony. He's not feeling well. The headaches don't stop. Is there no end to this horror?*

"Thank you. We'll do that." Jim never thought he'd be visiting the Chebucto School himself after he told Ted what it was used for.

"Would you like to see the baby? The nursery is this way." She pointed down the hallway.

Ted and Jim took a deep breath, looked at one another, then back to the nurse and nodded simultaneously.

"Dad, I'm glad the baby's alive, but I feel terrible about Uncle Carl, Aunt Liz, and my cousins. It's not fair." Ted felt like he was in a scene from a movie. It didn't seem real and it was hard to believe they were actually dead. *Dead, like Mr. Camden, like that lady on the street, like my Rebecca and her mother or Gerald's sister.* A sob escaped from his throat.

"I never should have yelled at Carl." Jim wrung his hands.

"Yelled at him?"

A half-smile crossed Jim's face. "You know, he was kind of a pain in the neck. He started projects and never finished any of them."

"What projects?"

"Like the time I apprenticed for a cabinet maker. Carl often borrowed my hammer, screwdriver, or plane. He never ever put them back. I didn't mind him using my things, but I like my tools orderly."

"What did you do?" Ted perked up. This was a side of his father he'd never heard. Usually his father was good-natured and even-tempered

"I got angry. I yelled and cursed at him."

Ted laughed, but it came out high pitched, and they both burst into laughter. "What did Uncle Carl do then?"

"He apologized and promised to put them back but never did. He was a good-hearted guy though. Always laughing. Not a mean bone in his body." Jim's eyes filled with tears but he quickly he pulled himself together.

When they got to the nursery they were led through rows of cribs. When the nurse stopped, they peered into the small bed that contained a tiny infant with fuzzy yellow hair, wrapped in a pink blanket.

"Is that her?" Jim asked.

The nurse nodded.

At the sound of Jim's deep voice the baby awoke. First she stretched her arms, kicked her feet out, and opened her eyes to reveal clear blue marbles, like her mother.

Jim held his breath. "Precious angel," he said. "Look at her. She's the image of Liz."

Ted was reminded again about the little shoe he'd found that first day. *What happened to that baby? Was this…? No, of course it wasn't.* But he couldn't help himself as he reached for the child's tiny foot. He felt dizzy and clutched the side of the crib. The infant looked directly at Ted and smiled a toothless grin.

Brushing away a tear, Ted concentrated on the petite survivor who melted him in that moment. This precious child had come to heal his heart.

"It was amazing," said the nurse. "She was found buried under the rubble but didn't have a scratch on her. They figured the overturned crib and blankets protected her." She wrapped the child again then picked her up. "Would you like to hold her?"

Jim nodded and gathered the little bundle to his chest. He pressed a kiss on her cheek, as he swallowed the large lump that formed in his throat. "Hello, Mary Elizabeth. God love you. How beautiful and happy you are. And you don't even know what happened to your mama and daddy." He swallowed again and looked at the nurse. "What happens to her now?"

"If there is no surviving family, she'll be placed in the orphanage."

Jim spoke with panic in his voice. "I can't let that happen. She's my brother's daughter. We'll care for her."

"Miss Jones told me that you are related, but we'll need proof of identity. It's wonderful you want her."

"Of course we want her. She's all that's left of my brother and his family. How can we not take her home with us?" Jim handed the baby to his son, then pulled out his handkerchief and blew his nose.

The nurse changed the subject. "I'm sure Miss Jones can help you. We've had trouble getting the baby to drink from a bottle. My guess is she was breast-fed. We tried a number of formulas until we finally found one she likes. I'll get a supply, diapers, and a warm blanket. I'll bring them out to you."

Ted put his face next to the tiny miracle and inhaled her pure sweet aroma. "You are beautiful," he murmured. Somehow this baby seemed to fill the terrible hole created in his heart when he wasn't able to save Mr. Camden, or when he found the woman and the baby shoe, but most of all when Rebecca died. He rocked the child gently and soon she fell back to sleep. They walked out into the hallway to find Miss Jones.

Doctor Munroe came out of a room marked X-RAY. "What are you doing here, Jim? Why, look at you. You look like you got into a fight with a tiger."

"I wish it had been a tiger instead of a building, but I'll be fine." Jim explained the circumstances of their hospital visit.

"I'm truly sorry." He put his hand on Jim's shoulder. "Too many died."

He hesitated a moment before he continued. "But are you okay?"

"Dad, tell him about your headaches."

"Headaches? What about headaches, Jim? How long have you had them?"

The doctor repositioned his glasses, moved closer to Jim and looked into his eyes. "You probably sustained a concussion. How long has it been?"

"Since the explosion, but…"

"No buts. I need to see you. I'll be in the office, Thursday. Come by in the morning. We'll need to do a thorough checkup. Take it easy. Go home; lie down. Must run. I'm headed to the OR. Glad you're taking the baby." He peeked at the child. "She's a beauty. Good luck."

Ted nodded goodbye as the doctor disappeared around the corner. They were interrupted by Miss Jones. "You're looking for me?"

"Yes. We want to take the baby home. I'm her uncle. My wife is a nurse and a wonderful mother. The child won't lack for attention at our house."

"Good. I'll need identification and you'll have to sign release papers. I'll get them."

"Dad, do you think this is a good idea? Don't you think we should ask Mother first?"

Jim smiled. "I know your mother pretty well. She'll be pleased to care for the baby."

"But you already have one headache; I think you're asking for more trouble."

"You know, for the first time since the explosion my head isn't bothering me."

"Well, just the same, we'll see if we can get a taxi home."

Miss Jones returned with the release. Jim read the papers and signed in the designated place. "By the way, Doctor Munroe can vouch for us." He picked up the parcel containing formula and diapers from the nurse.

"I can't wait to see Mother's face," Ted said with a smile, then spoke sadly. "I really am sorry about Uncle Carl and..."

"I still can't believe it. I want to think it's a nightmare and that I'll wake up soon. When you consider how many died, it's bound to affect us. Still, it doesn't make the heartache go away, does it?"

"No, Dad, it doesn't."

Chapter 15
The Newcomer

Caroline dashed to the window when she heard a car drive up before realizing she couldn't see with the boards blocking the view. She raced to the kitchen door.

"It's Daddy and Ted."

A sense of dread came into Martha's thoughts. *If they took a taxi it's because of Jim's headache.* She hurried to open the door.

"They've got bundles." Caroline was excited, she loved surprises. "Ted, what do you have? Let me see." She gasped. "A baby? Where'd you get it? Is it a boy or a girl?"

"Wait, Caroline," said Ted trying to be patient. "Let Dad explain."

Jim closed the door. "We went to see about Carl and…" He shook his head and swallowed hard, barely able to speak.

"I'm so sorry, Jim. I know you loved him. We loved them all." Martha put her arms around her husband, nodding as he told her.

"Carl and Liz, and we think both boys were killed although they couldn't find little Kenny." Jim broke down and wept.

To take the focus away from seeing their father so broken, Ted took a deep breath and announced, "But by some miracle this little one survived without so much as a scratch. Everyone, this is Mary Elizabeth O'Neill." He held the child out for them all to see.

Martha reached for the little bundle. To her it felt fragile, yet warm and it smelled so lovely. She pulled back a corner of the blanket and smiled at the precious little gift from God.

Caroline set the puppy down and crowded her mother. "Let me see. She's pretty. Her eyes are so blue. What color's her hair?" Lifting the blanket from the infant's head, she whispered. "Blonde? She sure doesn't look like any of us."

"No, dear, she looks just like her mother for whom she was named."

"Can we keep her? I promise I'll take care of her. It'll be fun to have a baby girl for a change."

"Caroline, that's not nice. She's a baby, not a puppy. Besides, we're very happy with our boys."

"I know, Mama. That's not...I just meant we've got three boys. I've always wanted a sister."

Jim patted Caroline's head. "That's fine. Now you have one. And I must contact my own sisters to let them know, don't you think so Martha?"

"Yes, Jim. They must be notified right away."

Ted spoke up. "But Dad, the telephone lines are still down. I can go to Portuguese Cove tomorrow."

"We'll both go."

"No, Dad. I'll go. Doctor Munroe said..."

Martha turned to her husband. "Doctor Munroe? Did you see him?"

"Yes, he was at the hospital."

"Did he check your eye? Did he say anything about your headaches?"

"Ummm."

Ted intervened. "We saw Doctor Munroe in the hospital hallway. I told him about Dad's headaches. He wants to see Dad on Thursday. Dad has to rest and not run all over town."

"Is that true, Jim? Did he suspect a concussion? Didn't I tell you that you should rest until you felt better?"

"Yes, dear, you did but there are so many things to do. There's time..."

"Enough!" Martha raised her voice. "You can't possibly go anywhere in your condition. Now if you don't want to go to bed you must relax in your chair." Her voice softened as she touched his arm. "Darling, if you don't take care of yourself then who will help us?" She nudged her husband toward the parlor.

"Caroline, take Daddy's coat."

"I can go to Aunt Maggie's, Dad." said Ted.

"Between the two of you I won't get out of here in a hurry. Let me at least write a letter to my sisters then you won't have to tell them. I'll get started on it right away. Maybe tomorrow we can identify the bodies."

"I'll get your stationery, Daddy," said Caroline as she hung his coat neatly on the hook.

"Let's see. Where can we put this little miracle?" Martha thought aloud.

"I know just the thing...be right back." Ted headed for the stairs and his room where he pulled out the bottom drawer of his dresser. *Just right for a baby,* he thought. He removed the sweaters and placed them in the drawer above, then carried the makeshift bed downstairs.

"Here you go, Mother. This should work."

Martha laughed. "You are inventive, Ted." She reached to caress his face. "You're so like your dad. This will be perfect. Caroline, would you like to hold Mary Elizabeth while I get bedding for her crib?"

Caroline beamed as she sat in the big chair in the parlor. Martha placed the bundle in her arms. The boys gathered around and oohed and aahed trying to make their new sister smile. Little Charles giggled when he saw her. A baby always seems to bring joy to a family.

The next few days were busy ones for Martha and her mother as they attempted to bring a sense of normalcy back to the household. Mary Elizabeth seemed to adjust well to all the attention she received from the other children and Charles was fascinated by the "bebe."

"Sometimes I think we have a little Frenchman here in Charles," said Grandma. "Don't you think so, Martha?"

Martha smiled. "Yes, he does speak with a definite French accent."

Caroline assisted with the baby and was a great help with the other children as well. She was patient and played games with them often making them laugh. Between a new baby and Mrs. Boudreau's puppy, the O'Neill household bustled. Caroline taught Allan how to feed and care for the puppy whose paws were healing nicely.

Allan's hearing was slowly returning but Martha still wanted him to be checked by the doctor.

Chapter 16
The Doctor

It was just a week after the blast that Jim and Allan got to see Doctor Munroe. Walking down the street toward the harbor they saw workers still busily cleaning up remnants of the horrific explosion. Power and telephone service were restored to some parts of the city; sidewalks repaired. Surviving buildings were in the process of restoration or demolition. And carpenters replaced the window glass at the O'Neill house.

Dr. Munroe's office was in a Victorian-style house on a side street that appeared to have escaped major damage. Of course the windows had been blown out by the concussion but had already been replaced. The doctor was just closing his office door when the two arrived. He invited them in.

"I nearly forgot you were coming. Don't tell me this is our little Allan? He's either losing weight or he's stretching out." The kindly doctor turned to the boy. "Do I have to patch you up? Have you been sliding down the back stairs in a dishpan again? You're going to have permanent bumps on your head, young lad."

Jim chuckled. "No, Doc, this time it's his ears. He's had difficulty hearing since the blast."

The doctor motioned for Allan to climb up on the examining table, picked up his otoscope and looked into the boy's ears. "Can't see much except a little wax. Maybe the concussion of the blast shifted it enough to create his hearing loss." He looked up at Jim. "Let me flush his ears, perhaps that will help."

The doctor proceeded to pour warm soapy water into a small basin. Then he took a syringe, filled it with the solution and flushed the boy's ears.

Allan looked up in surprise and said with a grin, "I can hear you!"

Doctor Munroe smiled back at the boy. "Well, no wonder. You should see all the potatoes I dug out of there. Okay, hop down. You're next, Jim. Tell me what happened."

Jim sat on the table as soon as Allan hopped off. "Henry and I were taking down the boxing ring when the place collapsed. I think I'm all right though. It was just a bit of glass and a beam or two."

"A beam or two? Hmm." He put his hand to his chin as if contemplating. "I guess that explains all the cuts that appear to be healing well. And the headaches? Do you still have them?"

"Yes. The pounding in my head is constant."

The doctor took Jim's blood pressure then looked into his eyes with a scope. "You've injured your right eye and it looks like you still have shards in it."

"My wife removed a piece of glass." Concerned that the doctor might want to remove his eye like they did to so many others, he said, "I think it's getting better though."

"Just the same, I'd like you to see Doctor Harrington. He specializes in eye injuries. Now, about those headaches. You said a beam hit you? My guess is you probably sustained a concussion. I want you to have an x-ray."

"I don't want an x-ray. Just give me something for the pain."

"Okay, here's medication for your headache but you'll have to take it easy for a few more days, Jim, to give your skull a chance to heal itself. No heavy lifting. The medicine will make you more comfortable. If you're not better by Monday I want you back here. We'll wait on the x-rays."

"Sure, okay. And how are you doing, Doc? What's the news and have you had a chance to catch your breath?"

"Did you hear that the first ship, the *Imo* was washed up on the Dartmouth shore while the second one, the *Mont Blanc,* simply vanished?"

"Really? That's incredible."

"Yes, the anchor was found more than three miles away in Richmond. I guess nearly every building on the west slope collapsed like a stack of cards, while others burst into flames. They estimate that 1,800 people died in that very moment."

"That's where my brother Carl lived. Guess I'm not surprised. It was unbelievable...the devastation. I never thought an explosion could wipe out a whole city."

The doctor nodded. "We've had some relief though. We Haligonians are extremely self-sufficient. Shortly after the blast, they organized search and rescue parties and were at work among the wreckage, digging out the dead and injured. By four o'clock the fire department had the ship blaze under control. Except for a few isolated areas that continue to smolder, most fires have been extinguished.

"Providing aid for the injured, shelter for those homeless and food for the hungry was the first concern. But Halifax was not alone as offers of money and relief poured in from other parts of Canada and from all over the world. It's amazing because within a few hours of the explosion we heard that a train with medical staff and supplies was on the way from Boston. New York City sent cots, blankets and food."

Jim slid off the examination table. "What an outpouring of generosity. I'm glad they could get through so quickly. Guess the railroad tracks were unharmed."

"I think some of the tracks were uprooted but when word came through that trains were headed this way crews were sent to repair them immediately."

The doctor picked up his bag. "I'm off to the hospital now. Oh, I nearly forgot. How's the new addition?"

"She's doing just fine. She'll be spoiled before the month is out. But that isn't the only addition at home. Our neighbor, Mrs. Boudreau, broke her hip and we are caring for her dog."

The doctor chuckled. "Good for you. Allan, here's medicine for you too. Take one a day. You might give one to your brothers and sister although the baby's too young just yet." He smiled as he gave the boy a handful of lollipops.

"Thanks, Doc. I appreciate your seeing us."

Allan was an animated chatterbox and talked all the way home.

"Everything was a jumble of noise in my ears. I saw some kids crying but I couldn't understand them and my ears hurt so much I thought they'd burst or maybe even fall right off. I was scared, Daddy. Then Caroline came for me."

He told his dad how they were only a minute late for school, how he rushed in and started to remove his coat when there was a loud noise and he was flung across the room onto a pile of coats. He told his father how when he scrambled to his feet his classmates and the teacher had formed a line to leave the building.

Jim hugged his son. "I'm glad you're okay now, little buddy. I was really worried about you."

Allan looked up at his dad with a feeling of importance. "Were you, Dad?"

Chapter 17
Headlines

When newspapers once again appeared on the newsstands Jim picked up the *Halifax Gazette*:

> December 16, 1917
> HALIFAX DESTROYED;
> DEATH TOLL MOUNTING; MANY DEAD,
> MORE HOMELESS; WHOLE FAMILIES
> WIPED OUT. Fire engines raced to the scene along
> the waterfront as the concussion sent a tidal wave
> swamping many boats in the harbor. At first there
> was a fireball, estimated to be as hot as the
> temperature of the sun.

"Martha," Jim set the paper down. "That's hard to believe."
Although stunned, Martha was fascinated. "Read on," she said.

> Even though the fireball lasted only a fraction of a
> second it was long enough to incinerate many people
> standing on the dock. The ground shock caused
> building foundations to weaken, making them more

vulnerable to the blast of air moving away from the center of the explosion with the strength of several hurricanes.

Jim stopped in amazement. "Is that possible? Why this is worse than we thought. I usually think of air as soft and gentle, like the first warm breezes of spring, or maybe even a wild wind like in a blizzard, but this was diabolical at seven hundred miles an hour!"

Wide-eyed, Martha put down her dishtowel. "Seven hundred? My goodness! I can't imagine it. What else?"

"It doesn't say how many people died but I heard it was over a thousand."

"Oh, Jim, I can't bear it. Those poor families. And it's so cold. Do you suppose we could put up some of them here?"

"Martha, Martha. You have enough to do with taking care of me, your mother, little Mary Elizabeth, as well as your own five children and the dog. I'm sure that when Mrs. Boudreau gets out of the hospital you'll want her to move in until her own house is rebuilt. Sweetheart, you have the softest heart imaginable." He smiled before continuing to read aloud.

The day after the explosion a train from Boston arrived laden with doctors, nurses, medical supplies and equipment. A cargo steamer came from Massachusetts Eye and Ear Infirmary with supplies and more help. A relief train from New York City followed with hundreds of cots, blankets, cases of disinfectants, as well as food. The generosity of so many countries was overwhelming.

"That's truly amazing. People are good-hearted, aren't they, Jim."

"Doctor Monroe commented on that. They sure are, dear."

Ted came into the kitchen. "Is that a newspaper? Can I read it when you're finished?"

"Of course," said Jim. "Here, take it. I was just reading it aloud to your mother."

Picking up the paper, Ted scanned the headlines and continued down the page.

> In their wild panic, the people of Halifax fled their homes and stores, leaving them unguarded and unlocked. Soon looters were at work turning over the wreckage and rifling the corpses.

Pouring a cup of coffee, Ted sat at the table, devouring the news. "Captain Mahoney told me there'd be looters. I'm glad I put the jewelry into locked drawers." He sipped his coffee. "Say, I heard the army is putting up tents as temporary shelters in the Commons. I'm going over to see if they need volunteers; that is, unless you have something you need me to do, Mother."

"No, dear, I think it's wonderful of you to help. I'm sure they can use strong men there."

Ted finished reading the paper, set his coffee cup in the sink, and said goodbye as he put on his warmest jacket, hat and gloves. When he approached the Commons, his heart raced. *I don't know if I can do this.* He straightened up. Aloud he said, "They need help. I've got to do it."

Huge piles of splintered wood from destroyed homes were unloaded from trucks and used as fuel for fires to keep the soldiers warm while they erected tents. It wasn't long before word got out and the displaced flocked to the Commons, or as some renamed it, *Tent City*. Ted handed out warm blankets, army surplus clothing and food.

Sparks flew as the wind blew fiercely. The army commander was afraid the tents might burn and ordered all fires to be extinguished. However, despite the order, most were re-ignited to provide at least a little warmth. By nightfall the wind died down and the area took on an eerie appearance as tents, illuminated inside by kerosene lamps, became translucent while the exterior was outlined by the flickering flames of bonfires. This macabre effect was accented by the glow of the burning harbor and haze from the smoke.

Some gathered around the fires wearing ragged clothing; others were wrapped in army blankets, a few clad in army greatcoats. All were huddled against the cold, pondering their profound loss. They suffered shock and grief, guilt-ridden because they were alive while loved ones perished. Ted tried his best to comfort some, which helped to defray his own grief. Yet every so often the sound of anguished sobbing pierced his soul. *I know I'm luckier than these poor people. Most have lost everything. At least I still have my family even though Rebecca...* He gulped down the lump in his throat and looked around. A young boy, perhaps seven or eight years old was shivering uncontrollably. "Hey there, what's your name?"

"John David Thornton."

"Hi, John David, my name's Ted." Ted took off his scarf and wrapped it around the young lad, and as a second thought gave him his gloves. They were too big for the boy but at least they would warm his hands. The boy looked up with great tears in his eyes. Ted felt compelled to put his arms around him to stop his shivering. "There, there, John. You'll be all right. I'll get you something warm to drink."

Most of the survivors were in a state of shock. They simply stood like statues; unseeing, unhearing, unfeeling, in silence.

Ted sat by the fires during the night talking with several soldiers, a wool blanket draped over his own shoulders. As dawn lightened the eastern sky he and some of the soldiers went to each of the tents announcing that fresh coffee was ready but soon discovered another horrible scene. More than a dozen people had frozen to death in their tents.

"We can't let these people stay here another night. We've got to do something," said the mayor when he arrived later in the morning. "We must utilize every vacant facility for housing; schools, warehouses, empty railroad cars, for these desperate citizens. Get started on it right away."

One of the soldiers urged Ted to go home and get some sleep. "You can come back later if you want."

Ted plodded back home. The snow had spread a pristine blanket of white over the blackened ruins. Truly beautiful at first, it was short-lived as later in the day the weather again became a vicious enemy. More than fifteen inches of snow swirled and drifted. Where it converged with heat from smoldering wreckage it turned to slush, then quickly froze as it ran down and away from the fires. Before long the ruins were sculptured in ice, making rescue work even more difficult.

Chapter 18
A Snowman

Once he arrived home, Ted found Caroline and Allan trying to shovel the front walk.

"Hey guys, what're you doing? You should be building a snowman. This stuff is too heavy for you. Let me do the shoveling."

"Jerry wanted to do it but of course Mama wouldn't let him outside with crutches. And Daddy is back in bed with another headache."

"Gosh, that's too bad. I'll be right out." Ted ran into the house and grabbed another pair of gloves.

"Here, let me have the shovel. You and Allan try building a happy snowman. We all need some cheering up."

"I'd say that's a good deal," said Caroline. She poked her little brother. "Come on, Allan, help me."

Ted widened the path his siblings had started. When finished, he helped with the snowman. It felt good to be doing something fun. His mind was still filled with the events of the past few days and it was hard to feel positive, but now he felt like smiling. *I have the best family and it's good to know Allan's hearing is back. I just pray Dad will get better.*

"Ted, can you help me with the snowman's tummy? It's too big for me. I can't lift it," said Allan, struggling with a huge snowball.

Ted went to him, rolled the ball toward the snowman and lifted it on top of the first part. He looked at his sister. "How are you doing with the head, Caroline? Looks like it's just about the right size. Want me to put it on top?"

"Yes. I'll go ask Mama for a carrot for his nose."

"Ask her for a hat too," called Allan.

Ted and Allan patted and prodded the snowman until it was just right. Ted looked down at his little brother. "What are we going to use for buttons?"

"I'll see if I can find something," said Allan.

Caroline came out of the house with a colorful scarf and a carrot. "Nice, but that isn't the scarf Grandma made, is it?" Ted asked.

"No, silly, it's an old one of Mama's. She said I could use it. Look what I have for the eyes." Caroline held out her mittened hand to reveal two plump prunes.

"They are just right."

Allan came back with half a dozen small rocks. "Can we use these for buttons?"

Caroline looked up after putting the snowman's eyes in place. "They're perfect."

Ted thought, I should have brought John David here. He'd get along well with my siblings. Then he looked up at the kitchen window. "Wait right here." He went into the house and in a few minutes came out with Jerry clinging to his back. Jerry reached over and placed a pipe in the snowman's mouth. "How's that?" He grinned.

"Jerry, it's perfect. We didn't think about a pipe."

When the snowman was completed they stepped back to admire their creation. Just then the kitchen door opened and there they were; Mama, Grandma and little Charles all smiling at the beautiful snowman.

Chapter 19
Mass Funeral

The sun felt warm and the air smelled clean on March 9. The entire O'Neill family were to attend a special funeral service outside the Chebucto School. Jim hired a horse and wagon filled with hay. Martha added quilts and blankets as they all piled in.

"This is fun, Daddy. I'm glad we could ride in the wagon," said Allan.

They picked up other friends and even strangers along the way. Jim and Martha thought it would be a good way for them to say goodbye to those they lost and to try to bury their own grief.

Cardinal William Carty arrived from Toronto, attended by his entourage. Father Maurice Boulanger of St. Michael's parish and Reverend Farmington of St. Luke's Episcopal Church were in charge of the impressive ecumenical service. Clergy from surrounding towns attended as well. A city councilman introduced the cardinal who spoke about the tragedy.

When he finished, a voice emanated from the choir: *"Coming, Lord. Oh Lord, I'm coming home today. The journey is over and Lord I'm coming home to stay."*

The soprano voice was clear and rang true as the first verse was sung *a capella*. Then a violin joined, harmonizing softly, verse after verse. The choir sang several hymns; *Come Gather 'Round, The*

Rugged Cross, Amazing Grace and ending with *How Great Thou Art.*

At first only a few people joined in the singing, then a few more and before long most everyone sang. Tears streamed down the faces of the mourners as well as the singers. Tears of sorrow, tears of heartbreak, tears of healing.

Then just before the two hundred still unclaimed dead, their coffins gathered and loaded onto trucks for Fairview Cemetery, officials were notified that the cemetery would not accept unidentified bodies. Instead they were to be interred in the city's potter's field.

A long procession of wagons, bicycles and pedestrians followed the convoy to Potter's Field. Again, prayers were said by the clergy and once again the crowd sang, *"What wondrous love is this O my soul, O my soul."*

When at last they dispersed, Jim followed the truck containing the coffins of the nuns from St. Mark's School who had been identified. They were buried together at Mount Olivet cemetery, their names listed on a single headstone. Ted placed flowers next to the grave and whispered to his mother, "Isn't this where our little Bertie is buried?"

"Yes, our family plot is there," his mother said, pointing. "We'll go over when we are finished here."

Chapter 20
Surgery

Jim's headaches continued to be so debilitating that he frequently took to his bed, requesting the drapes be closed, as light seemed to worsen the pain. His right eye had become badly infected. At Martha's insistence, Jim agreed to call Doctor Harrington.

On the day of the appointment, Martha accompanied her husband. Approaching Victoria General Hospital on the north side of the city, Jim became apprehensive. Once inside he regretted having come at all. His fears were allayed, however, when Doctor Harrington, a sixty-year-old man, with a shock of white hair, bushy eyebrows and a friendly demeanor reassured him. He shook hands with the couple, asked about their situation at home, how many children they had. He kept up a stream of conversation as he led them down a long corridor and into a small room. He motioned for Jim to sit in the examination chair after turning on a powerful overhead light.

The doctor peered into Jim's eyes. "I'm putting drops in your eyes to dilate the pupils and make it easier for me to see into the eye." He administered the drops. "It will take a few minutes. I'll be back shortly," he said, leaving the room.

Jim seemed anxious. He hated being fussed over and knew that Martha would find out that he was already blind in one eye. He anguished about it. "I don't want them to remove my eye, Martha, I don't want to be a one-eyed, a one-eyed, oh I don't know what. God, help me!"

Martha put her arms around her husband. She sympathized with this brave man. If only he'd seen the doctor sooner. But no, if he'd gone on the day of the explosion, they might have removed the eye then. At least now he has a chance. And maybe there are medications that can help.

"I need to tell you something, sweetheart," said Jim. As he was about to speak, the doctor returned. He spent a long time examining Jim's eye, all the while keeping up a stream of non-essential chatter, most likely to put the patient at ease. When he was through he shook his head. "I'm sorry, Jim, but there's still glass in there and your eye has become infected."

Martha reached over and took Jim's hand. "Can't you remove the glass, give him something to clear it up, Doctor?"

"We can try but I think the infection's gone too far. It has already invaded the vitreous humor, the clear fluid that fills the interstices. And, Jim, as you are aware, you've already lost sight in that eye. I'm afraid sepsis or blood poisoning will set in. If that's the case, we'll have major problems."

Martha looked at her husband in shock. "You didn't tell me that you couldn't see. You should have said something."

"Sure wish the news wasn't so grim," the doctor continued, "but I feel pretty certain we'll need to remove your eye."

Martha gripped Jim's hand tightly. Her worst fear was this scenario.

Numb and impatient, Jim growled. "Do it then. Get it over with."

"Not so fast, Jim, there's still time. First we need to arrange for a vacant surgical room. That may take a few days."

"Never mind then. I'll be fine."

"No sir, you wait right here." The doctor left.

"I'm so sorry, dear. I prayed that it wouldn't come to this."

"I'll be fine, Martha. Let's just leave now."

"No, dear, you can't continue like this. If the infection gets into your

93

bloodstream you could die. Don't take that chance. You can't do that to us. You have responsibilities to your family. Besides, we need you." Martha voice softened. She dabbed at the tears in her eyes. Jim started to argue but stopped short when the doctor returned with a smile.

"Look, there's a vacant room right now. We can do it immediately."

Noting Jim's hesitancy he leaned over and spoke sternly. "Listen, Jim, it needs to be done. I know you don't want it done. I wish to God there was another way, but there isn't. I can do it today."

Jim opened his mouth to protest but Martha spoke up. "That's fine doctor, he'll have it done today." She said it so emphatically that Jim simply stared at her.

The doctor sat on a stool. "So here's the plan. In the surgical unit we'll anesthetize the eye. Then with a sterile saline solution we'll flush out the remaining splinter or splinters of glass. I'm not too hopeful, but if the infection is localized to the area of the glass shards, we'll continue flushing the eye to see if we can possibly arrest the infection. However, if it has spread and I think it has, we'll need to remove the eye."

Doctor Harrington anticipated the look of horror on Jim's face. "Not to worry, you won't have a gaping hole, Jim. We have an array of artificial eyes and will select one to match your own green eyes. Why a friend of mine who had this same surgery claims he can see better with the glass eye." He winked. "Of course he's a joker but you've already adjusted to having the sight in just one eye." The doctor stood up to leave. "In just a few minutes an attendant will come for you. I'll get ready."

When the doctor left Martha moved closer to her husband. "Jim, we need to pray."

"You're right, my dear, we do need to pray." The two knelt down beside their chairs, their hands clasped tightly, and prayed, *"Our Father who art in Heaven..."*

As they finished an attendant entered the room. "How soon before they begin," Martha asked as the attendant motioned for Jim to sit in the wheelchair.

"It will probably be an hour or more, Mrs. O'Neill, but we have to prep him so we'll take him now."

"Darling, I need to let Mother know." Martha wrapped her arms around Jim and kissed him tenderly. As she left to find a telephone, she said, "I'll be back before they start the surgery."

She hung up the telephone after speaking with her mother and went into the chapel. Reaching into her purse for her rosary, she began to pray once more.

Tears flowed down her face and onto the crystal beads, a wedding gift from Jim. Sunlight streamed in through a stained glass window and glistened on her rosary. As she sat back in the pew, fingering the beads, her mind strayed. She thought about her wedding and how she first met Jim.

She was in the nursing program at Mount Olivet Hospital School. One day, however, while eating her lunch in the park a handsome young man sat on the bench next to her. He tipped his hat and she smiled at him. After a few days it became a ritual. One day Martha offered to share a dessert she had bought at the bakery earlier.

"Why, thank you," he said. "My name is Jim. Jim O'Neill. And yours?"

"Martha Johns. Do you live around here?"

He smiled. "I'm staying at the Robie Street Apartments temporarily but I'm from Portuguese Cove. And you?"

"I'm studying here at the hospital. I graduate in June and plan to return to Prince Edward Island to work at the hospital there." Martha told him a little about herself then asked, "What about your family?"

"My father's family came from Cork, Ireland and settled in Portuguese Cove. Besides my parents, I have two sisters and a younger brother."

"That's nice. What are you doing in Halifax?"

"I'm working on the remodeling of Simpson's Store."

Just then the clock in the tower struck one. "Oh my, I must get back to class."

"Thank you for the dessert, Martha. Can we meet here again tomorrow? I'll bring a treat."

"That would be nice." Martha could feel her face redden. This man was handsome and so polite. By June Jim had proposed and Martha changed her mind about returning to the Island. She wrote her parents who were aghast that their daughter would become involved with someone they didn't know. They wondered about him; his family; what kind of people they were.

One weekend Jim accompanied Martha to Prince Edward Island to meet her parents. They liked him immediately. On another weekend Martha visited Jim's family in Portuguese Cove. She fell in love with the entire family and they in turn loved Martha. Jim's sisters were so friendly that Martha felt she had known them all her life. His parents were nice as well. Jim's brother was in the service overseas so she didn't get a chance to meet him until just before the wedding.

Following graduation Martha and Jim were married at St. Patrick's Church in Halifax. The day was hot and sunny but a breeze from the harbor made it pleasant. Martha's gown of Swiss embroidered organdy was topped with a veil fashioned with yards and yards of tulle and Chantilly lace gathered at the crown and adorned with tiny white deutzia blossoms. The crystal rosary beads which she carried sparkled when the light glanced off them. Her bouquet was of white roses with a cascade of stephanotis.

Anna, her best friend and maid of honor, wore a gown of dusty pink taffeta and she carried pink roses. Jim's brother was best man and Martha's father walked his beautiful daughter down the aisle.

A reception was held in the garden next to the church. It was an intimate wedding attended by family and a few friends, which was typical in those days.

The newlyweds rented a small apartment in Halifax. Two years later, Ted was born and four years after that Caroline. When Jerry came along the apartment seemed to burst at the seams and they bought the house on Quimpool Road.

Martha left the chapel and returned to the waiting room where she found a seat. She looked up in time to see Ted rush in. "Oh, Ted," she managed to say before slumping to the floor.

Noticing the commotion, a nurse hurried over. Martha quickly regained consciousness as Ted helped her back into the chair. "Are you okay, Mother?"

"Yes, I just feel a bit weak. I'm so concerned about your dad. Did you know that he is already blind in that eye?"

The nurse brought over a glass of water and handed it to Martha.

"Thank you, I think I'll be all right now."

"Mother, are you sure? Grandma told me. Is Dad going to be all right?"

"Oh, dear we surely hope so. Ted, I'm so glad you're here." She patted to a place on the bench. "Please, sit next to me for a moment before we see your father."

Chapter 21
Rebuilding

After the long and brutal winter, signs of rebirth finally emerged. Repair and reconstruction efforts were everywhere as were the signs of nature. At first crocus, daffodils and tulips opened their buds, then lilacs and forsythia bloomed and finally cherry and apple blossoms burst forth in fragrant glory. Lawns turned a brilliant shade of green. Birds chirped. Fluffy tailed squirrels chattered. At last spring had arrived in the newly resurrected Halifax and the city was starting to live again.

Ted grew restless and fidgety. So many places and things still reminded him of Rebecca, of Mr. Camden, of the many bodies he uncovered and the pitifully few people who survived. He was anxious to finish his apprenticeship and get away from the nightmare of it all.

"What will you do now, Ted?" Mr. Young asked. "You know you're more than welcome to stay on part-time. I wish I could hire you full time but business isn't what it was before the explosion."

"I understand, sir. I'm not sure what I want to do. I love working here. You know I'm practically obsessed with clocks and their workings. Mother wants me to go to Boston where my uncle offered me a job in his ship scaling business."

"Ship scaling?"

"Yes. My father told me they overhaul ocean liners. He remembers two big ships there which they scraped and painted the last time he visited. Dad thought it was pretty amazing but it doesn't sound like anything I'd be interested in. However, I may try it, just for the experience and maybe I can save money to start my own jewelry business."

"Let me know what you decide, Ted."

"Thank you, sir, I will. See you tomorrow. G'night." On the way home Ted kept seeing reminders of that frightful day in December and of the heart-wrenching weeks that followed. Now, stores had taken on a new appearance. Simpson's, where Rebecca worked, looked modern, not at all like the original store. He passed by the florist where he'd bought her corsage. It was now a milliner's shop. There was no florist there.

Ted felt panicky. *I want to leave. I have to leave. I'll go out west, far away from here. Nothing to keep me now. In a few weeks I'll have finished my apprenticeship. Even though I like the work, there are no jobs here in Halifax, at least not in the watch repair or jewelry business.*

He passed a payphone, stopped momentarily, then went back. He picked up the receiver, inserted a nickel and called Gerald Keddy.

"Can you meet me downtown? Okay. See you then." As he hung up the telephone, his mind came up with all kinds of plans. *We could go out west, where there are real cowboys. Gerald and I often talk about how it must be on the prairie. It'd be a good change for us to get away from the gloom of this city.*

On Saturday night, Ted approached his parents. "Mother, Dad. I've decided I want to travel this summer. I want to find out what this country is about. I have a little money saved and can always work if I need to. I'll keep in touch, I promise."

Martha was stunned. "We thought you might leave home when you finished your apprenticeship to attend university, but I didn't expect you'd leave Halifax altogether."

Before Jim had a chance to speak, Martha looked at her husband, then her son. "I think this is something your dad and I need to discuss in private. We'll talk about it with you tomorrow, after church."

She had to mention church. *Guess that means I'll have to go, whether I want to or not. But she's not going to talk me out of leaving, that's for sure.*

On Sunday Ted sat with his parents at the kitchen table to discuss his future. Pouring coffee, Martha asked, "If you leave, where will you go? What will you do?"

"Out west. There are cattle ranches there. I'm sure I can get a job as a ranch hand. You know, herding cattle, putting up fences, that kind of thing."

Jim put his cup down. "Your Uncle Ed offered you a job in Massachusetts."

"I know, Dad, but working on a ship in the harbor doesn't sound like much of a challenge. Now if it were on the ocean...well, that might be a different story."

"Why do you want to leave Halifax, Ted?"

"There's nothing here for me now. Mr. Young doesn't have enough business for a full-time position and to be honest, I'm sick of this place. Everywhere I go, I remember how it was before the explosion and how gruesome a day it was December 6. I don't know if they'll ever repair the clock tower and I have so many memories of Rebecca. I hate it. I really hate it."

"We can understand how hard it is having lost Rebecca, dear," said his mother, "but you certainly don't have to go to the ends of the earth. Why, the west is...well, it's wilderness. At least in Boston you know Uncle Ed and we'd know you were safe."

Ted chuckled then said quite seriously, "Mother, I'm a grown man. I need to be on my own. This is what I want to do." He looked at his father. "What do you think, Dad?"

"I don't know, son, I certainly would feel better if you were closer to home. I understand you want to be on your own and that's fine. But so far away and not knowing anyone or anything about the area."

"Gerald is coming too. We'll be fine."

Martha stood up and put her hands on her son's shoulders. "Dear, we'd like you to wait another year before you do this. I think that with the trauma you've been through you need to be close to family. I don't think you should go just yet."

Becoming frustrated, Ted turned his back on them, not wanting to see the hurt in their eyes. He knew he wouldn't stay. He merely wanted permission so he could leave with their blessing. *I am leaving. I can't possibly stay here another year. Too many memories.*

"We'll talk about this another time," announced his mother.

Ted knew that when his mother made up her mind, there was no sense even trying to change it. Ordinarily she went along with most things, but not this time. Meanwhile, Ted went ahead with his plans, but his parents never did change their minds. One day Martha noticed that her son had packed a duffel bag.

"What in the world are you thinking? I thought we decided you'd wait a year."

"Mother, you decided. I'm not waiting. I'm leaving today."

"But you can't…" she called as he opened the door.

"Goodbye, Mother."

Chapter 22
A New Venture

Gerald was already waiting at the train. "You all set? You look like crap. Have you changed your mind?"

"No, I haven't changed my mind. It's just that my mother and I had words. I hated leaving in the heat of an argument but...well she wouldn't listen to my side. I'm not a kid anymore."

The ride was a long one and the boys alternately dozed and watched the scenery as they chugged from Halifax across to New Brunswick then over the river bridge and into Quebec. They could see the great fortress surrounding the city. It reminded Ted of the Citadel in Halifax and he didn't want to be reminded just then. He was glad they were just passing through. Absorbed in thought, he spoke very little.

"This is pretty nice," said Gerald, running his hand over the upholstered bench seat where they watched the landscape flash by. The train rocked back and forth as it sped along the tracks and the boys slept soundly. Over mountains, down into the valley, across the plains through Ontario and Manitoba then finally days later they arrived at their destination, Regina, Saskatchewan.

Ted looked around. "Where are the trees?" he asked. Everything seemed strange. The buildings were a completely different architecture from what he was used to and even the people, the few people there were dressed like something out of the western movies he saw at the Embassy Theatre.

He nudged Gerald, "I thought they wore those clothes just for the movies. I didn't know that's how it really is."

"I know what you mean. And boy, isn't it hot," he said fanning his face with his hand.

Ted pulled at his shirt where it stuck to his back. The hot, dry air seemed to suck the life out of him.

On the wall outside the station was a poster, which read:

HELP WANTED.
Must be strong and willing to work.
Room and board provided.
Call Tom Garvey at 4478

"We have to find a telephone," said Ted.

"Hey, maybe there's one in the hotel. Let's find out." Gerald flung his bag over his shoulder and started to cross the street. Ted did the same. The hotel interior was ornately decorated in red and gold velvet draperies. It smelled like a combination of perfume and tobacco. It wasn't unpleasant, just different. A plush sofa was positioned near the window with several large potted plants and a spittoon in the corner. An older gentleman sat behind the reception area. A uniformed bellhop stood at attention beside the desk.

"Do you have a public telephone?" Ted asked.

"Over there," the man said, pointing toward the lobby.

Ted had memorized the telephone number and gave it to the operator. He waited until finally someone answered and then cleared his throat. "Hello. Is this Tom Garvey?" Ted looked over at Gerald who was anxiously pacing.

"This is Ted O'Neill. My buddy and I saw your advertisement. Yes, we can start right away. Halifax. Two. That's right. Yes, yes. Okay, thank you. Bye."

Ted frowned as he hung up the telephone then lowered his head pretending to be sad. "Well, buddy, the job's been taken."

"Oh crap, just when we had our hopes up." A sly grin appeared on Ted's face. "Hey, are you serious? Tell the truth."

"Yep. The job is ours. We just have to wait 'til this Garvey guy comes for us. Meanwhile, let's take a look around."

Ted thanked the receptionist as they left the hotel. Along the street were several stores and a barbershop. They passed a feed and grain store, then a ladies' clothing shop, a saloon and finally came to the general store. Ted noted how two men sitting outside the store were dressed; big cowboy hat and boots. "Hmm," said Ted. "We may have to buy new clothes."

"Let's go in."

"I'm going to buy a hat." Ted tried one on. "How d'you like this?"

Gerald laughed. The hat was several sizes too big.

They tried on quite a few hats before they each found one they liked. Next they tried on boots and chaps, picked up two plaid shirts and brought them to the counter.

"D'you find everything you need?" the clerk asked.

"Yes, thank you." Ted reached into his wallet. "What does it come to?"

"Let me see." The clerk jotted the prices on a piece of brown paper and totaled them up. "Twenty-two dollars."

Ted gulped. He looked at Gerald who started to remove money from his wallet as well.

The clerk saw the expression on their faces and quickly added: "No, no, that's twenty-two for everything. Eleven apiece."

They smiled at each other and whispered, "That's better." They paid the man.

"We'll wear the hats," Ted said. "We're going to work on the Garvey ranch."

The clerk turned around, reached up on a shelf and gave them each a red bandana. "You'll need these. It's pretty dry and dusty out there."

"Oh, thanks. How much?"

"Nothing. I know you'll need them and you'll most likely be back here a time or two. Good luck to you both."

"I like your hat," said Ted to Gerald who strutted like a peacock.

"Like yours too."

Although the boys were tired from a long arduous trip, they were excited now about their new adventure and hoped to earn lots of money. "Looks like our ride is already here."

As the truck pulled up beside the hotel, the boys grabbed their bags and packages. They called to the driver who stepped from the truck.

"Over here. You Tom?"

"Naw, I'm Hank. Toss yer things in the back and hop in." The driver was tall and lanky with a cigarette dangling from the corner of his mouth.

The boys did as they were told and were off to see a new world. Their driver had few words to say as they rode over the bumpy, dusty road. "Guess that guy knew what he was talking about. I'm glad he gave us the bandanas."

"Me, too," said Gerald.

Chapter 23
Cowboys

At first Ted and Gerald enjoyed living in the bunkhouse with real cowboys. They learned to smoke cigarettes and even drank a little, sometimes a little too much. A tremendous headache the following day reminded them that it wasn't worth it to get drunk. The other ranch hands, all older, laughed at the greenhorns but soon had respect for them when Gerald asked to borrow a guitar, tuned it and began to strum. He and Ted sang, harmonizing on the chorus. Ted made up a song about Rebecca, which brought tears to the eyes of the cowboys. They learned other songs from the ranch hands. Some were about long lost love and others were raunchy ditties.

When one of the guys asked about the weather in Halifax, Ted said, "Well, you know it's real rough in the winter. Our home is up on a hill and there's a brook that runs right through it. At the end of the brook is the barn. Of course we have to feed the animals, even in bad weather." Ted looked at Gerald and winked.

"Here it comes," mumbled Gerald.

Ted continued. "In the winter the fog gets so thick we have to wear our fog shoes."

"Fog shoes?" inquired Hank.

"Yeah, you know, they're sort of like snow shoes. You have to lace them up. First we have to pry open the window, then step out and flog to the barn in our fog shoes."

"Wow, that must be something," exclaimed one ranch hand. "I never even heard of them. Of course, we don't have fog out here where it's so dry. Why, you guys can do the darndest things. I've even seen the way you ride horses. You're pretty good."

Gerald smiled, remembering how he and Ted often rode two horses at once, with one foot on the back of each horse. Sometimes they rode bareback and slid down around the neck of the horse and came up again on the other side. They had a wild time.

Ted kept his promise to write to his family.

> *Hello everyone,*
> *It's pretty hot out here on the prairie. We swim in a pond after work and the water is really cold but it feels good after a long day. Gerald and I are becoming experts at rounding up the herd. Gerald plays the guitar and we sing to entertain the other ranch hands at night. Guess that's all for now. I hope everyone is fine. Give hugs to all.*
> *Love, Ted*

He told a fib about rounding up the cattle but wanted to sound like he had a good life in the west. He didn't want them to know how disappointed and even homesick he was. It was hard and boring work. Each day they looked forward to doing a little *cowboying* like learning to lasso a dogie or rounding up cattle. But those things were chores for the older men.

Gerald and Ted had to do the dirty work. They mucked out stalls, fed and watered the farm animals, then loaded gallons of water onto the truck. Hank drove with the boys in the back. It was a long haul to the herd. They'd had a dry spell and needed to supplement the water supply. Sometimes they spent long days repairing fences under the hot sun. There was little shade on the prairie. No trees, only a few tumbleweeds that got in the way. They both agreed that the one good thing about being hot and sweaty was the icy cold pond they jumped in at the end of a long day.

One evening, some of the men went into town for supplies. Afterward, they stopped in the saloon. One guy got pretty drunk and started to pick on Gerald, calling him a herring choker and worse. "Hey, Jack, that's enough," said Gerald.

"Whadda ya mean enough? How about this." And he punched Gerald in the stomach. Of course a fight ensued. Ted, who also had a few drinks, got into the fray. He never fought much before and surprised himself that he did as well as the others even though he ended up with a bloody nose.

The bouncer kicked them out. On the way home, Gerald exclaimed, "Hey, Ted, I didn't know you were a fighter."

"I didn't either but I sure was mad." Ted held his red bandana to his face. "God, I think that creep broke my damn nose."

The next day there was a letter from his father.

> *Dear Son,*
>
> *We're glad that you're enjoying your summer. It has been hot here too. The Arena is repaired now but I still suffer headaches and cannot do the manual work. I left that job to take another just across the street at Greenwood's Grocery. It is much easier, but I love the Arena and will miss the skaters. Henry was promoted to manager. I promised to show him how we make ice come November. Oh, he's helped me at times, but he needs to know the entire procedure. I also told them I'd go over at night to sharpen skates for the hockey pros. He said they would appreciate that, as I am the best sharpener around. That made me feel good.*
>
> *Jerry's leg is better. He and Allan are running and there's a race next month they want to enter.*
>
> *Caroline helps your mother with the babies. Little Charles is walking, still holding onto the*

*furniture but I don't think it will be long before
he's off on his own. And you wouldn't believe
Mary Elizabeth. We decided it is too a long name
for such a little one. Now we call her Elizabeth.
She is crawling all over the place and loves to tip
over the dog's water dish. Yes, we still have the
dog. Mrs. Boudreau is here too. She continues to
have difficulty walking.*
   That's all the news for now. We miss you.
   Love, Dad.

Ted felt lonely after reading and re-reading his Dad's letter. His father's penmanship was something to be admired. Each letter was formed perfectly with a flourish. It truly was a piece of art. It seemed that everything his father did was perfect. *Wish I could be more like him. Ever since the explosion I've a hard time doing what's right. Never used to fly off the handle like I did with Mother or even Gerald at times. Guess I'll have to try harder. This independence isn't what it's cracked up to be. Maybe I will go to Boston to work on the ships. I'll to talk to Gerald tomorrow about quitting here.*

Chapter 24
Summer's Over

By the end of August the boys had their fill of being cowboys. They quit their jobs and began the long hitchhike home. There was little traffic so they walked a lot. However, luck was with them because on the second day a trucker stopped and drove them all the way to Niagara Falls.

Gerald continued on home but Ted wasn't yet through with his sojourn. Actually, he dreaded going home to face his mother and the memories of Rebecca. *At least there are days here when I don't even think about her. Wonder if you ever get over loving and losing someone? I think about her but not nearly as often as I used to. Guess we worked too hard on the ranch. Maybe hard work and distance has helped after all.*

Ted decided to buy a motorcycle with his savings instead of trying to hitchhike. He headed south through White Plains, New York, and eventually to Boston, Massachusetts.

"Well, well, what have we here?" bellowed Uncle Ed when Ted showed up at his office.

"Thought I'd see if I could get a job here in the States."

"Why sure. I'm looking for help but I want to warn you, it's hard work."

"I'm not afraid of hard work, Uncle Ed. I've been busting my butt all summer."

"Okay, you can start on Monday, but first come on home with me. Aunt Sally will be delighted to see you."

Uncle Ed and Aunt Sally lived just outside of Boston in a two-story home with beautiful gardens leading down to the Mystic River. It was serene there, a complete change from the dry prairie. And to top it off, a thunderstorm was brewing.

"Hi, Auntie," Ted said as he walked into the house.

"My glory, Ted. I'm happy to see you. You look so tan. Have you been out to sea?" She threw her ample arms around her nephew.

Ted hugged his aunt and laughed. "No. And certainly not on vacation either. I've been working on a ranch out in Saskatchewan. It's hot and dry there. This rain feels wonderful to me."

"I'm glad you're here," said Uncle Ed. "Come, I'll show you to your room. You might want to wash up for dinner, and then we'll call your parents to let them know you arrived here safely."

The delicious meal of roast beef and potatoes reminded Ted of his mother's Sunday dinners. Ted didn't want to talk to his family just yet. "Thanks for dinner," he said. "Hope you don't mind but I'm really tired. Think I'll sack out, oh excuse me, go to bed." *Uncle Ed knows I'm not ready to speak with Mother just yet.*

"Of course, you've had a long journey," said Aunt Sally.

Ted crawled into a bed with the fresh crisp sheets. *Didn't realize how hard those bunks were. This is like sleeping on a cloud. And the food, it tastes so good.* He dreamed he was back home. Suddenly a darkness came over the dream and Ted awoke, frightened. *What was that about?* He got up, took a shower and put on his last clean shirt and pants. *Better find out if I can do my laundry.* As he started down the stairs Ted heard his uncle's booming voice and smiled. The man was actually singing first thing in the morning.

"Good morning," said Ted, entering the kitchen.

"Well, good morning yourself. Did you sleep well? Are you hungry? Ready to go to work?"

"Yes to everything, Uncle Ed."

"By the way, I think you'll need to drop the *uncle* when we are at work. Ed is fine with me."

"Good morning, Ted. I've made scrambled eggs and bacon for you."

"Aunt Sally, thank you so much. It smells delicious."

The car windows were open on the way to work with Uncle Ed. Ted could smell the salt air as they neared the shipyard. He inhaled and suddenly was reminded of home. "The salt air reminds me of Glassy Island. I don't think you ever saw our summer house, did you, Uncle, I mean, Ed?"

"No, I'm afraid we never got up there in the summer. What was it like?"

"We had a fireplace, big enough to burn a railroad tie. The house sits just beyond the apple orchard. We'd pick wild blueberries and blackberries the size of my thumb. Of course we ate nearly as many as we picked. When we brought our containers to Mother, she made the most wonderful pies you could imagine."

"I know she's a great cook, just like my mother," said Ed.

" I can almost smell the pies now, fresh from the oven, their juices bubbling over the crust. If we were really lucky, it was served with a heaping scoop of vanilla ice cream either Dad or I made earlier."

Ted continued his memories of home. "You know, we'd often see deer race across the open glades in the woods, especially in early morning and again at dusk. And most every day we'd go to Bedford Basin to swim or fish. The water was usually cool and refreshing but sometimes it got really cold. That's when we'd see the seals, their little black heads bobbing around in the waves. We fished for lobster, clams, and eels and often caught haddock or codfish for dinner.

Sometimes when we were out and about, we'd catch a few trout and cook them over a fire, just for a snack."

"What a great time you kids must have had. Guess you miss it?"

"Yes, I do in many ways. We'd use whatever conveyance was available, usually a rowboat. Another family lived nearby and they had an old Swedish boat. It had a deck on top and we'd have dances there." *What a life,* thought Ted. *We had the best of everything.*

112

The sounds of gulls, men shouting over the din of the trucks and other vehicles, brought Ted back to reality just as they pulled up at the dock. In front of them were three large ships.

Butterflies gathered in Ted's stomach when he saw men on scaffolding over the side of one of the ships, scraping away like they were just inches off the ground.

"I don't like heights much. I was pretty skittish when we worked on the clock tower although the view was something else. When you looked down toward the basin, you saw the stores, the streets, the docks and the boardwalk. We saw so many ships, big ones and smaller ones too. And if you looked up the hill, well there was the Citadel with its cannons ready to protect the city."

"Halifax is a wonderful place, Ted. Here we are." Ed introduced Ted to one of the men he'd be working with.

"Rob, you show Ted what to do." He looked back at his nephew, nodded his head and told him to go with Rob. Ted held out his hand. Rob shook it then described the task at hand.

Looking up at the side of the ship he explained: "First we check over the entire ship to estimate the work to be done. Then, starting in the prow we scrape and sand until all blistered and chipped paint is removed. Next another crew comes through. They prime the sanded areas. After that a third crew applies paint to the entire ship and before you know it the ships looks brand new."

He motioned for Ted to follow him up the gangplank. "We have work to do here as well. The brass has to be cleaned and polished and a fresh coat of shellac applied to the teakwood. Then the deck is scrubbed until it is practically white."

Ted was assigned to polishing brass. It reminded him of how he often polished a piece of jewelry at Young's Jewelry and Repair Shop. He felt homesick for all the timepieces in that shop. *I really love the business. Maybe one day I'll go back to it.*

Ed was proud of his nephew who was an excellent worker. After nearly three months he approached him. "Well, Ted, do you like this kind of work? Is it something you want to do for the rest of your life? You know, one of these days I'll want to retire. Maybe you'd like to take over the business."

"I like what I'm doing right now. I love the smell of the sea and much prefer this climate to what we endured out west, but as far as a career, I don't think so. Eventually I want to get back to what I was trained for, namely clock and watch repair."

"Well, hell. Why didn't you say so? I know a man who has a little shop on Mass. Ave. His health has been failing. I think he's looking to sell the business. Is that something you'd like?"

"Before the explosion I thought about opening a shop in Halifax. I never thought about moving somewhere else but it's what I love to do. Do you know how much it would cost to buy his place?"

"No, but I'll find out. By the way, there'll be a bonus in your pay envelope this week. No need to say anything about it. I've been watching you and you've been an exemplary employee."

"Thanks, Ed...Uncle Ed. I've been able to save my money because you won't take anything for room or board. I do think I'd like to own a shop here in the Boston area. Maybe I have enough money to start."

"Perhaps you could work with this ailing man until you come to a price agreement."

"But my tools, they're in Halifax."

"So go home and get them. And better make amends with your mother while you're there. When you come back we'll talk business."

Chapter 25
The Homecoming

Ted went back home the second week in December. Still mild during the day, the nights were cold. Nearly bare of leaves, many trees still showed a collage of red, orange and gold. It reminded Ted of the time Caroline left her crayons on the radiator. He smiled with the memory. His stomach was full of butterflies as he entered the house, but there was no need. His mother welcomed him with open arms. He had apologized earlier in a private letter to her. The family was overjoyed to see him.

Caroline had blossomed into a real beauty, Jerry was nearly as tall as Ted and Allan was no longer chubby. He too had shot up. Charles was a busy toddler and Elizabeth looked adorable with her deep blue eyes and blond hair.

Grandma was Grandma, beautiful as ever. Her pure white hair glowed like a halo in the light. His dad seemed frail and his mother had lines in her face that Ted had not noticed before. *Has it been that long?* He wondered. But they all were happy to see him and he was glad to be home.

Downtown Halifax was still rebuilding. His father had managed the Arena for eight years. He loved working there as it was close to home and the pay was enough to support his family. It was too much for him now and he had taken a job at Greenwood's Grocery. His heart was still at the Arena, however. He had devised a unique method of sharpening ice skates called a hollow grind. Normally skates were sharpened with the grind going across the blade but it caused rough ridges. Jim ground it parallel to the blade making a very fine grain. Only the edges touched the ice. After the blades were sharpened, he rubbed them until they were smooth as glass. The oilstone he used was indented where his fingers had held it.

Many pro-hockey players believed they skated faster when Jim sharpened their skates. When he was satisfied with the blade's sharpness Jim packed the skates into straw-lined barrels and shipped them back to wherever they came from; Montreal, Quebec, Ontario or even the United States. Besides being expert at skate sharpening, Jim was also adept at ice making. When days and nights dropped below freezing he'd attach a hose to the spigot and flood the rink. Some people turned their hoses on full blast to make ice, but Jim used a fine spray. Next he opened the shutters under the bleachers which created a cross-flow of air beneath the floor. The water froze solid. Although it took longer to prepare, the ice was far superior. They'd have ice from November to late March, providing an excellent place for hockey games, family ice skating and ice carnivals.

The evening Ted arrived, Caroline set the table with the damask tablecloth and used the good china. Mama was cooking a roast of beef while Grandma took care of the little ones.

"Are you going to stay?" asked Allan

"No, I don't think so. I want to open my own watch shop in Boston. Uncle Ed knows of one that'll be available soon." He looked around. Everybody looked sad. "Hey, cheer up. I'll be back and you can visit me once I have a place. Who knows, I might even hire you for the summer."

Their faces brightened. Ted changed the subject. "Tell me what you've been doing."

"We're back in school," Caroline said. "I have a wonderful teacher. And I'm taking art lessons."

"Great. You'll have to show me some of your work. And you, Jerry?"

Allan jumped in and said, "Jerry and I are racing."

"Racing? What do you race?"

"Bicycles," said Jerry. "You should see Allan go. He's the fastest."

"Really? That's great."

"And sometimes we go on the ice. Not with bikes, but skates. Daddy got Jerry a pair of racing skates. We're going to race this winter."

"Do you have racing skates too?" Ted asked.

"Naw, don't need them. I go pretty fast with my old hockey skates."

"We were talking about you the other day," said Caroline. "Remember that time you came to the rink? First people stared, then someone giggled and soon everyone was laughing."

Ted remembered. He wore baggy pants, a Derby hat and carried a cane. His black shoe skates had long blades. But people thought the funniest thing was the mustache, a la Charlie Chaplin. Ted trimmed the inside edge of Grandma's mouton lamb coat and used it as a moustache. When he got on the ice he went through silly maneuvers of slipping and falling. They all thought it was funny. All except Grandma who wondered about the mustache. She had noticed a patch of missing fur but thought that moths were feasting on her good coat.

"And 'member how we played the Victrola? I was good at winding it up," said Allan excitedly.

"I remember when your Dad and I had a New Year's Eve party," said Martha. "We put a record on and danced to the music. I happened to glance at the staircase and there you were, all of you lined up on the stairs to watch the party. I was about to say something but Dad whirled me around and whispered, 'Let them be.'"

"Thanks, Daddy. I'm glad you let us watch," said Caroline. "I remember how the ladies looked so pretty in their beautiful dresses and everyone seemed really happy."

Ted got into it. "Do you remember how I'd play the piano while you three marched through the dining room then past the piano and back into the kitchen? Each time you came by you carried a different instrument. First you all had pan lids and clashed them like cymbals, then Allan carried a wooden spoon and he beat on the big pot Jerry held."

"Oh, that was so much fun," said Allan.

"Playing this memory game, I seem to remember that every time we walked past the home of the Pugh family, you kids held your nose saying phew, phew," said Jim.

"But, Daddy," said Caroline, "it was all in fun and when we got to meet the Pughs we stopped doing that."

Ted stood up. "I hate to break up this party but I really should pack my things. I'm anxious to find out about buying that shop and starting a new career. First, I need to telephone Gerald. I haven't heard from him." Ted had been holding Elizabeth and now gave her back to his mother.

"Oh, Ted, can't you stay 'til Christmas? It's almost here. We've missed you so much," asked Caroline.

"I don't know. I'd like to be here for Christmas but...well, let me think about it. I have to get my tools packed anyway." Like his father, Ted took very good care of his tools; his jeweler's loupes, the small vise, pliers, long tweezers, mallets, polishing supplies, files and the engraver. Mr. Young had presented him with a case for his tools one Christmas. Ted wanted to be sure everything was in good order.

"Where's the telephone book, Mother?" He looked up the Keddy's phone number. It rang a few times before Mrs. Keddy answered. "Mrs. Keddy, this is Ted O'Neill. I'm fine thanks. No, just for a brief visit. Say, is Gerald home? Really? When? No wonder I haven't heard from him. Do you have his address? Thanks. How's Mr. Keddy? I'm glad. Tell him I send my regards and I'm sending you a hug from me. Thank you, Mrs. Keddy. I will. Bye."

He hung up the telephone and started up the stairs but stopped. "Mother, did you know that Gerald Keddy joined the Royal Mounted Police?"

"No. I hadn't heard that. Did you talk with him?"

"No, his mother told me. I think it's great. He'll make a good Mountie."

He hesitated before descending back down the stairs. He gave her a hug. "I have to pack a few things, then I hope to get a good night's rest. Good night, Mother. Good night all."

The telephone rang early the following morning. It was Uncle Ed. It seems that the owner of the shop they were interested in was taken ill so the purchase would be delayed.

"I'm sorry to hear that. But because there is a delay I'll spend Christmas here. I'll be in Boston before the first of the New Year. How does that sound?"

"That's fine, Ted. Now let me speak with your mother."

"Okay. Bye for now." He handed the telephone to his mother and went into the parlor.

"Guess what," he said. "I'll be here for Christmas after all so you'd better tell me what you want while I still have money in my pocket or you'll be out of luck."

Caroline told him she wanted a new paint box. Jerry asked for a book but Allan couldn't decide.

"You still have time to think about it."

"We have only two more weeks, Ted," said Jerry.

"Two weeks, eh? That's not much time, is it?" Even though there were still reminders of his loss, Ted was happy to be home. But he was deeply concerned about his dad who'd always been energetic and the mainstay of the family. Now he was but a shadow of the physical man Ted knew.

"Henry asked if I'd help sharpen skates tonight. There's a hockey game tomorrow and the boys want to be ready. Want to come along?"

"I'd like that, Dad. I haven't been to the Arena since it was repaired."

When they walked into the building the smell of the cold damp rink hit Ted. It felt good to be there and he wished he'd brought his skates. You'd have thought his father was a celebrity the way the skaters greeted him warmly and crowded around him. As soon as Jim picked up his tools to sharpen the skates, a change came over him. He practically glowed, so you knew this was his passion, being at the rink and sharpening skates to perfection. Ted smiled and thought, *I'm so proud to be this man's son. He's surely someone to be admired.*

The following morning Ted went to the clock repair shop and told Mr. Young of his plans. "Wonderful," Mr. Young replied. "You'll do well in your trade and I wish you good luck. Keep in touch. If I can ever help you out, let me know."

"Thank you, sir. I appreciate that."

Chapter 26
Tradition

"Dad, the boys want to help us pick out a Christmas tree this year. When can we go?" asked Ted.

"I don't know, son. I've been thinking, perhaps it's time you to took over that chore."

"But, Dad, you've always done it and for the past few years I've gone with you. Jerry and Allan want to come this year. It's becoming a tradition."

"I know, I know, but there comes a time when we need to start new traditions. It's time for you and the boys to take it over. You already know who to contact and where to go."

"I know your headaches are bothersome so if you don't feel up to it…."

"Please do it. I'd appreciate it."

"Okay, but if you change your mind, let us know."

Ted phoned for permission to pick out a tree at the Flanagan farm. "Come on, boys, put on your boots and warm clothes if you want to help. I've already sharpened the axe. Jerry, you can pull the sled."

"Don't you want to wait for Dad?" asked Allan.

"He said for us to go without him."

Jerry and Allan seemed disappointed their father wouldn't be coming with them. However, they felt grown up to finally help select the tree. It was a three-mile hike to the farm, and another trek into the woods to select the perfect specimen.

Ted thought. *There isn't much snow for the sled. If Dad were with us, he'd have come up with another solution. He might even suggest we carry the tree rather than dragging it. If we keep to the side of the road, there's probably enough snow.*

When the O'Neill boys arrived at the tree farm they spoke with Mr. Flanagan and went in the direction the man indicated.

They hadn't gone far when Allan jumped up and down with excitement. "I like that one," he said pointing to a tremendous blue spruce.

"It's too big for our house," laughed Ted. "Let's keep looking." *I loved it when Dad and I came here. It was a special time for us. Guess I'll have to try to make it special for my brothers, but I sure wish Dad were here.*

They looked at tall trees, skinny trees and fat trees until they found the right one.

"Are you sure this is the one?" asked Ted.

"It's perfect," the boys shouted in unison.

With that, Ted handed the axe to Jerry. "You take the first cut, Jer, then Allan will have a turn."

Jerry, although tall and thin, wielded the axe like a pro and made the first cut. Next, it was Allan's turn. He had trouble hitting the same spot as his brother but finally took a good chunk out of the tree. Ted finished up and they yelled "timber"as the tree fell to the ground. The three of them lifted it onto the sled and tied it down.

Mrs. Flanagan came out of the barn as the boys were heading toward home. "Wait. Here's something to put on your door. Tell your parents we wish them a Merry Christmas." She handed Ted a big wreath decorated with partridge berries and cones.

"It's beautiful, Mrs. Flanagan. Thank you. We'll give your greetings to our parents. I'm sure they would say the same to you. Merry Christmas!" Ted carefully placed the wreath on top of the tree and gently slipped the end of the rope through it.

"That was nice of her, wasn't it?" said Allan.

"It sure was."

"Brrr, I'm cold. Wonder if Mama can make us hot chocolate," shivered Jerry.

"Me, too," echoed Allan.

Ted pulled the sled. "First we have to get home and put the tree in the shed, just in case it snows or worse yet, rains. We don't want to bring a wet tree into the house."

They took turns pulling the sled and when they got home they propped the tree against a wall inside the shed. Ted hung the sled on a nail, wiped the axe and put it in its place before they went into the house.

Sure enough, the table was set with the hot chocolate cups, along with a plate of sugar cookies Caroline and her grandmother had just made. It was a nice celebration to start off the holiday season.

"Should we let Santa decorate our tree as usual or do you think he'd appreciate a little help this year?" Martha asked.

"Can we really decorate it? It will be so much fun," said Caroline.

"We certainly can hang this up right away," said Martha admiring the wreath.

"I always liked the magical way our house was transformed when we awakened on Christmas morning," reminisced Ted, "and the beautiful tree adorned with lights, angel hair, glass balls and tinsel, with brightly wrapped packages underneath." Ted wondered how in the world his parents managed to do it all in one evening because except for their stockings which they'd hung from the mantelpiece before going to bed, there was no sign of a holiday. It truly felt magical.

"I don't think your dad is up to it this year," said Martha. "So maybe it's time to start another tradition and decorate the tree together."

"Mama, can we? Can we please? We've never decorated our tree before," pleaded Caroline.

Martha looked at Ted. He nodded. She smiled. "We'll decorate it Saturday."

Ted was glad they'd put the tree in the shed because on Friday night a fast-moving storm deposited a foot of snow. The boys got out their shovels and cleared the walkways as well as the driveway before bringing the tree into the house.

Caroline and her mother got the decoration boxes out of the attic. They hadn't celebrated Christmas the previous year because there were so many homes and stores to be repaired, as well as the enormous task of comforting of friends and family. They were anxious now to see if the ornaments had survived the explosion. Luckily, most of them were intact.

Once they got the tree into the stand and were assured it was as straight as it could be, Martha suggested that Ted string the lights since his father wasn't home from work yet.

"I'm so happy you're home, Ted. You did a fine job."

"Thanks, Mother." Ted smiled. He was happy to be home too. When the lights were on, Martha handed a box to the children who took turns hanging the colorful balls. There was a smaller box she kept for herself. In it were special ornaments; some from her childhood home on Prince Edward Island, some were gifts from her husband and others were made by the children.

Grandma handed the unbreakable decorations to Charles and Elizabeth and the older children helped hang them on the tree.

"Pretty," said Charles.

"Pitty," chimed Elizabeth. Everyone chuckled at their little mimic.

Martha whispered to Mrs. Boudreau, "How blessed we are to have such a loving family. I just wish that Jim could be a part of the decorating. He's in so much pain I think he'll appreciate it being done for him."

Mrs. Boudreau patted Martha's arm. "I know. I'm sorry."

When the tree was completed Martha stepped back to look at it and said, "I think this is the prettiest tree ever."

Ted laughed. "You say that every year, Mother."

"It's surely the most beautiful tree I've ever seen," said Mrs. Boudreau. "Our trees were always small and we had very few ornaments. I'm so happy to be part of this year's celebration with your wonderful family."

Martha stood next to Mrs. Boudreau and gave her a hug. "We're so happy you are here, dear. It means a lot to all of us."

Ted got up. "I'm going to my room. I have some wrapping to do, so no peeking." Admiring the tree he said, "I think we did a fantastic job!"

Martha shooed everyone out of the parlor and closed the door. "We'll keep the door shut so the little ones don't pull the tree down. And that goes for you too, Pumpkin Puppy."

By now the dog was no longer a puppy. She was a delightful interim pet for the children but Martha constantly reminded them that it was still Mrs. Boudreau's dog.

On Christmas Eve, Grandma stayed with the two youngest children while the rest of the family went to Midnight Mass. Afterward, they enjoyed the light meal she'd prepared. All except for Jim, who declined the food and went straight to bed.

Ted and Caroline cleaned up the dishes then hung their stockings by the fireplace. Eleven stockings adorned the mantel; one for each of the children, plus their parents and grandmother, Mrs. Boudreau and even one for the puppy, just right for a dog bone.

"Santa will be here all night just filling everyone's stocking," said Caroline.

"Don't you know it. Guess we'd better get to bed so he can get started." Ted winked toward his mother.

Chapter 27
Christmas Day

Early Christmas morning Allan jumped on Ted's bed, startling him. "Hey, what's going on?"

"Wake up, Ted, it's Christmas. Didn't you hear Santa's sleigh bells? Jerry and I did. Come on, lazybones. Get up."

Reluctantly, Ted pushed back the covers, put on his robe and slippers and followed his brother out to the hallway where they lined up in order of age.

Martha carried Charles and Ted took Elizabeth from his dad.

"Dad, you okay?" asked Ted. *He looks nothing like he used to. His skin is pale where it used to be ruddy.*

Jim nodded as they descended the stairs. When they opened the door to the parlor, they gasped. It looked beautiful and there were so many gifts under the tree. The stockings were filled to overflowing with oranges, candy and small gifts.

"It still looks magical," remarked Ted, "even if we did decorate it ourselves."

"You play Santa this year, Ted," said his mother.

"Okay." Ted was suddenly struck with the thought that this Christmas was very special. It took on a very different meaning. The gaily-wrapped gifts weren't nearly as important as family. A lump formed in his throat as he snatched a package from under the tree. "Let's see, it says to Caroline. No, it's Jerry. No, it actually says to Allan."

Allan quickly tore the paper off his gift and lifted the cover from the box. "Wow, skates!" He picked up one, inhaled the scent of the new leather and put the skate on his foot. "It fits. Bet I can beat everybody, now."

"Who's this one for? Can't quite read the writing."

"Oh Ted, you're such a tease," said Caroline with a big smile on her face.

Trying to be fair, he handed out the gifts giving one to each person in turn.

The last present under the tree was shabbily wrapped. He wondered who it was for. He picked it up and looked at the tag. It was rather heavy for such a small package.

"Here you go, Dad, this one's for you." He handed him the gift.

Ted noted that his father's hands trembled when he removed the paper to reveal the contents. Inside was a whetstone.

"It's from me," said Allan proudly, "the one at the Arena is all worn out. I thought you needed a new one. Besides, d'you think you can sharpen my new skates?"

They all laughed. "I certainly will sharpen your skates, Allan. Thank you, it's a great gift." Jim didn't tell his son that only through years of sharpening skates did his stone wear down so that it perfectly fit his hand.

Suddenly a muffled voice was heard. "DaDa, where Lilibet?"

They looked in the direction of the voice and there was Elizabeth, sitting under the tree with Allan's skate box on her head like a big hat. They burst into laughter once again as the little one raised the box off her head announcing, "Here me am!"

Grandma announced that breakfast was ready and suddenly everyone realized they were hungry, although they reluctantly left their presents to follow the aroma from the kitchen.

Christmas was a great celebration as usual, made even more special with the addition of Elizabeth and lots of laughter and love. Everyone got just what they wanted.

Chapter 28
Another Tragedy

Two days after Christmas, Jim was ill with vomiting and diarrhea. "Must be something I ate," he said staggering to the bathroom again and again. He was in there for a long time.

Martha was worried. "Jim, are you all right?"

The door opened and Jim stumbled out, white as a sheet. "I need to lie down."

"I'll help you, Dad," said Ted, taking his father by the arm, helping him up the stairs and into bed. "Can I get you anything, anything at all? Are you cold?" Ted pulled the blankets up to his father's chin.

His father moaned, pointing to his head.

"Your head again?" Ted moved to the window and drew the shades just as Martha came in with pain medication. When she saw how sick her husband was, she told Ted, "Call Dr. Munroe. See if he can come right away."

Ted ran downstairs to the telephone. When he hung up he said, "Grandma, the doctor is coming right over."

Grandma and Mrs. Boudreau kept the children busy in the kitchen making cookies. Ted ran back upstairs pacing and praying, watching his dad's every movement, every flicker of his eyelids. He checked the clock. Why aren't the hands moving? Although it seemed an eternity, in less than an hour he heard a knock at the front door. He dashed down the stairs, yanked open the door, shook hands with the doctor and pointed to the staircase. The two rushed to the bedroom, the doctor carrying his black leather bag. When they entered the room, Doctor Monroe flung off his coat. Ted grabbed it and placed it on a chair.

The physician put his hand on Jim's forehead and saw great pain in the man's eyes. "This is serious," he said, picking up his stethoscope. Just then, Jim slipped into unconsciousness. The doctor looked up at Martha and Ted. "It doesn't look good," he said, shaking his head. He bent over Jim again, checking vital signs.

"Can we get him to the hospital?" asked Ted.

"I'm afraid it's too late," said the doctor sadly, "he's gone."

Martha gasped and clasped her hands to her mouth to prevent a scream from escaping. Ted put his arms around his mother and pleaded in a voice filled with panic, "Speak with him, Mother, tell him not to die!"

Ted's mind spun violently. *This can't be. He can't die. He has a family to care for.* Memories from a year ago flooded his brain. He thought of the poor man in the repair shop, who also had a family to care for, but it didn't matter, he died anyway. And now his father…who was just forty-nine years old. Only later were they to learn that the cause of death was a blood clot to the brain. Ted left his mother and doctor in the room and numbly descended the stairs.

"Where's Grandma?" he asked, looking around.

"In her room," said Allan, a puzzled look on his cookie crumb face.

Ted knocked on the door where Grandma was folding the never-ending pile of laundry.

"Come in," she said. When she saw her grandson she knew by the look on his face it wasn't good news. She didn't speak. She didn't have to. Ted shook his head and went into her arms.

"Why? Why? Why?" Ted cried.

The children sensed something was dreadfully wrong and rushed into the room. Grandma bent down in front of the children. "We must pray." The children knelt in a circle. "Dear Lord," said Grandma, "take care of Jim. He has suffered so, let him be at peace." She looked at the children and told them that their father was dying. She didn't tell them he was already dead. They entered the circle of arms and wept openly with tears of great sadness.

From then on the family walked around the house as if in a trance. Every so often Caroline or Jerry or Allan might try to say something but a lump prevented the words from coming out and soon tears fell again. They couldn't help it, their feelings overflowed and it was contagious.

"Grandma, could you call Father O'Sullivan, please?"

"Of course, dear." She telephoned Saint Thomas Aquinas rectory and asked for Father O'Sullivan. Next she phoned Jim's sister.

Feeling the shock of the news Jim's sister Margie gasped. "Dear God, I can't believe it. I'll call Francine. We'll be there as soon as we can."

Ted took the telephone. "Thanks, Grandma, I can make the rest of them."

"Are you sure? I certainly don't mind."

"I'll do it." He called his uncle. They spoke at length, Ted trying to stay calm. Uncle Ed told him he and Aunt Sally would be there the following day. He called the Greenwood's, Henry at the Arena, and finally Mr. Young at the shop. He was exhausted when he hung up the phone.

Word spread quickly and within hours friends and neighbors dropped off baked goods, homemade soup, a freshly stuffed and roasted turkey and offers to help. The Greenwoods sent baskets of fruits, freshly baked bread and a large platter of cold cuts.

Father O'Sullivan arrived looking somber, a great contrast to his usually jolly demeanor. He'd baptized most of the O'Neill children and was often invited to Sunday dinner and other celebrations at the house. He felt a part of the family. First giving each a consoling hug, he went upstairs. When he came down, his eyes were wet with tears. He gathered the children in the parlor and told them their dear father had received the call to heaven and they were to tell him goodbye.

"Be sure to tell him you love him," he said, gently cautioning them that even though it looked like he was asleep, his soul was really with God in heaven. "Never again will he suffer headaches or any other pain."

The children spent time at their father's bedside, starting with Ted who knelt beside the bed. Tears he'd held back earlier came out in a flood. *It's not fair that this wonderful man had to suffer so.* When Ted opened his eyes and looked directly at his father, he saw that his demeanor was of serenity and calmness. He realized then that his father was at peace. He said a prayer, placed a kiss on his dad's forehead and left the room.

Caroline was next. She reached for her brother's hand. "Ted, can you stay with me?"

"Of course." He held her hand as they entered the darkened room.

When at last everyone had spent time with their father, Martha went in and closed the door. She was there for a long time. When she finally came out, the mortician and his assistant went into the bedroom and removed the body to be brought back later, after the embalming.

For now, Grandma was the strong one in the family as she went about the usual business of feeding and caring for them all. Caroline was helpful with her siblings and Mrs. Boudreau kept the dirty dishes to a minimum, washing and drying them practically as soon as they got to the big black soapstone sink. But it was Grandma who kept things on an even keel.

Allan and Jerry tried to be brave but tears streaked their faces too. Charles and Elizabeth seemed to sense the tragedy even though they were too young to understand. Both were unusually quiet and content to snuggle against anyone who'd hold them.

Chapter 29
Life Must Go On

The day passed quickly but Ted didn't want it to. He wanted to erase the pain and go back to a time before…before what? Before yesterday? His Dad was in pain then. Before the explosion? *True, we wouldn't have…I wouldn't have lost Rebecca, none of us would have experienced the heartbreak and pain of the horrific explosion. Then again, good things came from that tragedy. They had sweet little Elizabeth and by now it seemed like they'd always had her.* "Guess we just have to take what comes and face it day by day."

How will Mother go on without Dad, thought Ted. She depends so much on him. And my brothers and sisters, they still need a father. Oh, God, this is going to be hard on us all.

Ted was the self-appointed doorman. When anyone came, he greeted them, accepted their condolences and gifts of food and comfort and kept them moving. He didn't think his family should have to speak to everyone just yet. There'd be time tomorrow at the wake or the funeral. I need to protect my family from as much sorrow and hardship as I possibly can.

The aunts and uncles from Portuguese Cove arrived by late afternoon. Grandma and Caroline made the sleeping arrangements.

Grandma had moved into Caroline's room when Mrs. Boudreau came home from the hospital because the woman wasn't able to maneuver the stairs.

"You can come back to your own room, Anne," said Mrs. Boudreau, "the bed is large enough that we can share it."

"That's nice of you, dear, but Martha asked if I would stay close to her. She was there when my husband died and I really appreciated it. Thank you for the offer."

"My goodness, woman. It's your room. It's the least I can do." Mrs. Boudreau smiled.

Ted readily gave up his room. He and Caroline decided to bunk in with their brothers.

"I can sleep on the floor," said Allan.

"No need," said Ted. "I can squeeze in with you. It'll be warmer that way." Ted got up early the next morning. His mother and grandmother were already in the kitchen preparing breakfast. As he moved closer to hug his mother, a big lump formed in his throat. Ted swallowed but the lump wouldn't go down and soon tears spilled from his eyes once again.

"Don't you know it's all right to cry?" She put her hand on his arm.

"I know, Mother but I want to be brave for you…and the family."

"You'll do just fine, dear." Afraid she'd cry as well, Martha moved the coffee pot to the back of the stove. "For now, please let the dog out. She's whining at the door."

Ted stepped onto the back steps as the dog dashed out the door. The air was crisp and it felt good in his lungs. *I'm so confused. I want to do what is right but I also want to get on with my career. The timing never seems right.* A shiver slid down Ted's spine. He whistled and the dog came quickly.

Martha poured her son a cup of coffee then sat opposite him at the table. "David Hornsby said he'd be back by noon today to rearrange the parlor for the wake. Ted, can you help him? I know you'll make the right decisions. I can't do it, not just yet."

"Of course, Mother, I'll do whatever you want me to do."

Soon the kitchen bustled with children and relatives. Ted finished his coffee and went into the parlor. *How in the world are they going to rearrange this room? The Christmas tree occupies the whole corner and there's a lot of furniture here.* Ted thought about it and before he knew, Mr. Hornsby and his assistant were at the door.

"Come in," said Ted. "This way."

Mr. Hornsby was a tall, lanky and soft-spoken man who treated the family with utmost respect. "May I see the room where he'll be laid out?"

"Of course." They followed Ted into the parlor. Looking around, Mr. Hornsby asked, "Do you mind if we remove the tree?"

At first Ted felt shock when asked that question but he already knew it would be the sensible thing to do to make space for the casket. He hesitated for a moment then told the man of his idea. "I'd like to move it into another room."

"That can work although it will be difficult to move it without losing some of the ornaments," said the undertaker. "But we can try."

With the help of his assistant, the tree was carefully positioned in the dining room in front of the bow window. Only a bit of tinsel was lost on the way. Next, the men removed the sofa and big overstuffed chair, placing them temporarily in Grandma's room. They rearranged the other furniture to make room for the casket.

"Okay, I think we're all set. We'll be back in about an hour." With that the two men left the house.

Back in the kitchen, Ted took his mother's hand. "Come with me." He led her into the dining room.

"Oh, Ted, it looks beautiful." She hugged her son tenderly. "Thank you for keeping the tree. I was so afraid they'd have to dismantle it. I know your dad would be happy to have it here. Christmas has always been a special holiday for us. It looks lovely by the window."

"It does." Ted smiled at his mother.

The hearse pulled into the driveway. The men carried the coffin into the parlor and set it under the window. Folding chairs lined the walls. Baskets of flowers were placed on stands behind it with tall dim lamps on either side; a small bench as a kneeler in front.

"It looks fine, thanks," said Ted. He cautiously approached the casket that was now open. When he looked at his father he was taken aback. *He looks like he just closed his eyes for a moment.* Jim wore his glasses, his ebony rosary clasped in his hands. Ted said a prayer, gulped back tears and quickly left the room.

A loud knock at the door startled Ted. He opened it to Uncle Ed and Aunt Sally and greeted them with open arms and more tears as he led them into the kitchen. Martha was relieved that her brother was finally here. "It's a long drive from Boston," she said. "You must be exhausted."

"No, we decided to take the train," offered her brother. "We thought it would be easier and safer than driving as the roads are icy. And because we relaxed the whole trip we're not even tired. What can we do to help?"

"Just your being here is help enough for now," answered Martha.

Father O'Sullivan was in the parlor. He had nodded his approval when he walked into the room then knelt to pray beside the coffin. When he was finished he called the immediate family in. The priest had coached the children on what to expect.

Two by two, they again said their goodbyes to their father. Caroline was afraid to look up at first but was pleased when she did. It still looked like her father. She wasn't sure what to expect. Allan hesitated then reached in to touch his father's hand and whispered, "I love you, Daddy."

Martha took Charles by the hand and approached the kneeler. The little boy stood while his mother prayed. Then he looked at her, put a finger to his mouth and whispered, "Shhh, Daddy sleep." Martha nodded and smiled. She knew her husband would be proud of their youngest son.

Ted carried Elizabeth and when she saw the body she said, "DaDa." She wanted to get in next to him but Ted told her he was sleeping.

Other relatives as well as friends and neighbors came to pay their respects and expressed their deep-felt sorrow to the family. They sat in one of the many chairs that lined the room's perimeter until Mr. Hornsby urged them to go to the dining room.

A group of ladies from the church set up the prepared food on the dining table. The house was crowded but there was enough food to feed everyone. Once they had eaten, they stood in the hallway until the priest recited the rosary. Afterward most everyone left.

The day was an exhausting one. Nearly two hundred people had paid their respects to Jim and his family. Jim's sisters and their spouses left, promising they'd be back for the funeral. Martha's family would now occupy Ted's room.

It was late when everyone was at last settled into bed, everyone that is, except Uncle Ed who volunteered to tend watch over his beloved brother-in-law.

Chapter 30
What Next?

Ted fell asleep as soon as his head hit the pillow, but not for long. He kept thinking about his father and the family. Torn between wanting to open his jewelry repair shop in Massachusetts and feeling obligated to stay in Halifax to help the family, he tossed and turned, trying not to disturb his little brother.

Finally he gave up and went downstairs. A light was on in the parlor. He peeked in. Uncle Ed was sitting in a straight-back chair, his head in his hands.

Ted walked in and sat next to his uncle. "Are you okay?"

Uncle Ed sat up straight and blinked his eyes. "Guess I fell asleep for a moment."

"Uncle Ed, what do we do now? Since I'm the oldest I feel compelled to care for Mother, Grandma and the kids."

"It's not entirely your responsibility, Ted, we'll all help out the best we can. We can think about it for the next few days. Then I want you to tell me what you want to do."

"I already know what I have to do, Uncle. I have to find a job here in Halifax to support my family. They certainly can't make ends meet with the little money they have saved and no income."

"There's Summerhill. You could probably get a nice price for that property."

"Oh, no, we couldn't sell that place. It's been a wonderful retreat for our family. There the kids are free to fish and swim and…"

"That's true but let's be practical, Ted. At least you must think about it."

"I will. I'll try to come up with another plan before we have to sell it. Another thing, I don't think this is the time for me to be off to Boston to start a new enterprise." He hung his head. "I was really excited about having my own shop, but it just isn't to be. This isn't the time."

Afraid he'd appear feeling sorry for himself Ted stood up. Hearing a noise in the kitchen he left his uncle's side to investigate. Aunt Sally was busily making coffee and getting ready to whip up breakfast.

"I think we have some bacon too, Auntie." Ted went to the cold pantry and returned with a slab of bacon. Before long the aroma of bacon sizzling, toast toasting and eggs frying, as well as the delicious fragrance of the coffee brought the rest of the family to the kitchen.

Allan dragged the high chairs to the table and Jerry helped Charles and Elizabeth into them while Caroline got their bibs. Mrs. Boudreau appeared from her room and immediately began to set the table for the family.

Soon Mama and Grandma came downstairs. At first everyone was quiet and reserved but as cups of hot coffee were consumed and breakfast was served the family began to relax.

"Tell me about your Christmas," said Uncle Ed to the boys. "Did Santa come?"

"I got new ice skates," replied Allan. "I'll show them to you after breakfast."

Soon most everyone was chatting and even laughing over the antics of Elizabeth and Charles as well as remembering funny times and events of the past.

Suddenly, Caroline stood and indignantly spouted, "I don't think we should be laughing and having fun. After all, Our Father just died."

Getting up from the table, Uncle Ed put his big arms around the young girl. "It's okay to laugh, honey. You know your dad wouldn't want to see a bunch of grumpy faces around here now, would he?"

Caroline looked up at him cautiously, then smiled sheepishly. "Guess you're right."

"By the way Martha, Mrs. Brown from the Ladies' Sodality told me that they'd be here around two o'clock again today to help with the food," said Grandma. "I nearly forgot to tell you."

"The women from the church have been just wonderful. They're hard-working and so caring," said Mrs. Boudreau. "I've hardly had a dish to wash; they just took over and did it all."

"It's a beautiful tribute to Jim and the entire family," chimed in Aunt Sally. "You can tell how respected and well-loved you all are in the entire community, not just the church."

"I know and I'm grateful," said Martha.

"Mama, Grandma said we could work on a puzzle today in her room, that way we won't be in the way. We'll keep Elizabeth and Charles with us too."

"That's wonderful, dear."

Chapter 31
Closing a Chapter

Father O'Sullivan presided over the Funeral Mass on Tuesday morning. The church was full, a tribute to the respect and esteem in which Jim and his family were held.

The organ played softly in the background until the processional began and the priest came in from the sanctuary followed by an altar boy holding the incense burner. The casket, carried down the center aisle by six pall bearers, all friends of Jim was placed at the foot of the altar. The family came next. Ted assisted Martha, dressed in a black dress with matching gloves and a black mantilla covering her head. His grandmother, also dressed in black, held onto Ted's other arm and the children followed close behind.

Martha waited as the children filled the pew. Her mother sat with Elizabeth snuggled on one side and Caroline on the other. Martha sat next to the boys with Ted on the end.

The priest turned, bowed before the altar then faced the congregation and blessed them. "*In nomine pater, et filia, et spiritu sanctus. Amen.*"

Ted's thoughts kept drifting away. He knew how much the family would miss their dad. He blinked back tears and tried to concentrate.

After Father O'Sullivan had read the gospel he eulogized: "I have known the O'Neill family for many years. In fact, I believe I baptized most of their children. The death of their father is extremely sad. Jim was of a pleasant, quiet nature, an upright and honest man who was loved by all who made his acquaintance. His death is all the sadder from the fact that he leaves a widow and children. I know they have the sympathy of a large circle of friends."

In his heart Ted prayed not only for his beloved father but also for his dear Rebecca and the many other deaths he witnessed. It all came back to him once more. He wasn't ashamed of his tears as they were genuine. His siblings would be without their father; one who had always been there for his family, a man who was a wonderful role model and who made each of his children feel special.

The bells rang and Ted became aware again of the Mass as they knelt for the consecration. The choir continued; *"Sanctus, Sanctus, Sanctus."* Soon it was time for communion. Ted led his mother up to the communion rail. An altar boy placed the paten under her chin while Father O'Sullivan held up the wafer saying, *"Corpus Christi."* Placing the precious wafer on her tongue, he repeated this procedure with each communicant. Ted assisted his mother and grandmother back to their seats and held the babies while Caroline, Allan and Jerry received communion.

When Mass was over the funeral director motioned for the family to start the recessional. First Ted, then each family member in turn, lovingly touched the casket as they left the church. Interment was at Mount Olivet Cemetery where the family gathered around the graveside. Previously, with the assistance of a machine that first heated the earth, the men dug the hole into the frozen earth and a canopy and chairs were set next to it.

Ted shivered as he sat with the family. A sharp wind seemed to penetrate through his coat. He felt almost as cold as the night he went to The Commons.

As people gathered, the priest again said prayers and slowly the casket was lowered. Just then the wind died down and the sun came out. Everyone looked up and smiled at one another. It was a good sign and a number of people smiled as they stood to leave. Martha thought about her father when he was buried. The sun came out after the rain that day as well.

Chapter 32
The Future

Once back home the family sat around the kitchen table and talked about the Mass and about their father. There were no more tears, just numbness.

Ted walked into the parlor surprised to see it back to its original arrangement. When did Mr. Hornsby do that? He was relieved that the whole ordeal was over. It was an exhausting few days.

Aunt Sally excused herself from the table to pack. "We'll be leaving on the afternoon train."

Uncle Ed got up. "Martha, can you and Ted come into the dining room? We need to talk."

"Oh dear. Of course." Martha wiped her mouth on her napkin.

Ted followed them. When they were seated Ed told them what he had in mind.

"Look, I know it's soon but we have to talk. It is going to be a hardship for the entire family without Jim's income, Martha. Sally and I discussed this and we think that your life should go on as normal as possible."

Martha started to interrupt but her brother held up his hand. "Of course it seems your life can't be normal right now with the huge gap Jim leaves. He was a good husband to you, Martha, a great father to his children…just a wonderful man. We'll all miss him. What I mean is I don't want money to be an issue.

"Because Sally and I have no children of our own, we've agreed to subsidize your family. We'll contribute to the financial welfare of the O'Neills for one year. That way your lives can be as normal as possible. When the year is up we'll talk finances again to re-evaluate the situation."

Martha protested but Ed shook his head. "Let me finish, Martha. I'll need to know what it costs to run a family of this size. You know I've been lucky in my line of work. It would make me feel wonderful to share my good fortune with you. I've jotted some figures down but I need to know what Jim's weekly salary was and what savings you have. I know you own the house and your summer place. What else?"

Ed jotted down more figures. "Oh yes, and let's see, there are five, no six children plus you and Mother. I know Mrs. Boudreau is here just temporarily."

Martha wiped the tears that spilled down her cheeks and swallowed hard before she could speak. "Mrs. Boudreau insists on giving us money each month. She hasn't much but she said she'd feel uncomfortable if she couldn't pay something."

"And I've money saved from this past summer, Mother. I'll get a job here and help out as well," said Ted, taking his mother's hand.

Ed spoke. "No you won't, Ted. I'm sorry, but you have a career to build. You have a chance to start a business. I think it's a great opportunity in a field which you love and have had training. I know you'll need to stay here with your mother for a while but then you'd better get down to Massachusetts. It's fortunate there's been a delay in the purchase of the jewelry shop but it won't last forever."

Again Martha dabbed at her eyes with her handkerchief. "I think your uncle is right, dear. You need to go ahead with your plans. You know your father would hate it if he were the cause of you having to give up a stepping stone to your career."

Ted took a deep breath. "I know this is a chance of a lifetime, getting a shop of my own. The location is perfect and the price is right too but I can't go until I know that you and the kids will be okay."

"Ted, think for a moment about what your Dad would say." A sob escaped Martha throat. She couldn't stop the tears from coming no matter how much she tried. "I'm sorry," she said wiping her eyes and sitting up straight. "You know he'd urge you to go on, especially knowing that we'll be fine financially. My brother has made us a most generous offer. I think we should accept it."

Looking first at his mother, then his uncle, Ted said. "I don't know what to say. It all makes sense, yet...."

"It's your sense of duty that's holding you back and keeping you here." Uncle Ed looked at his notepad, nodded his head, then continued, "I believe this matter has been settled, don't you, Martha?"

"Yes Ed, I do and I'm so grateful for both you and Sally for helping us out. I just hope that one day we can repay your kindness."

"Are you kidding? Do you remember just how many scrapes you got me out of when we were kids on the Island? It is I who owes you, dear sister."

Ted left the room shaking his head. "I don't know about you two."

For the next few weeks Ted stayed with his family, spending time with his siblings, encouraging them to talk about their dad and going over finances with his mother.

One evening he received a phone call from his uncle. The shop owner was ready to sell. "You've got to get here right away."

Ted had mixed emotions. He was eager about his career. He knew the family would be able to manage financially, but he also felt especially close to his mother and siblings, closer than he had felt in a long time. He also knew he had to get on with his career, so after heart-wrenching tears and promises to write, Ted said his goodbyes and left for Boston.

Chapter 33
A New Beginning

The prospect of having his own place was exciting. With his uncle's help they plunged into setting up the shop to Ted's specifications. Almost immediately people came; some out of curiosity and others to have watches or jewelry repaired. A few even purchased new items. Ted was busier than he had been in a long time. "At last I'm doing what I was meant to do." He was happier than he'd been since the explosion. "Guess this was the thing to do," he mused.

Soon winter was over and before he knew there were signs of spring everywhere. Ted was excited when Aunt Sally pointed out the crocuses popping their colorful blossoms up from the warming earth.

It was shortly before Easter when Ted attended a jewelry show in Boston. He wanted to see the latest in watches and trends in jewelry and to pick up tips on how to display the various items. While there he noticed a tall, slender woman. She was fashionably dressed, her hair bobbed in the latest style. Ted walked over to her booth.

She looked up and smiled. "My name is Anna. Is there something I can help you with, sir?"

Ted gulped. Her voice was sultry and it took him by surprise. "Yes, I was admiring your display of jewelry."

"Thank you. Would you like to see a particular item?"

"No. Yes. I'd like to see that emerald ring." *My, she's absolutely gorgeous.*

It was the beginning of a new friendship in Ted's life and Ted was truly happy. After a few months a letter arrived from his mother telling him that they were going to Summerhill. "I'm somewhat apprehensive," she wrote, "but I think we should go, at least for this summer."

A few weeks later he received a note from Caroline.

> *Dear Ted:*
>
> *At first I hated being here because Daddy wasn't here and you weren't here either but do you remember David Thorpe? I met his brother, Thomas this summer. He's nice. Cute too. And he's not like most of the boys around who are often rude. No, Thomas, is really nice to me. We always have so much to talk about. Thomas says he's going to be an architect.*
>
> *Oh, Ted, I want to tell Mama about him but I'm afraid to. You know how she is. I don't know if she'd approve of me seeing a boy, never mind an Indian boy. Do you think I should tell her? Please write back soon.*
>
> *Love, Caroline*

"God, now what," said Ted aloud. "Mother will have a fit, I know she will. I don't see anything wrong with her seeing Thomas. The Thorpes are a fine family. David and I were good friends, in fact we're blood brothers. Long ago we made cuts on our wrists then bound them together so the blood intermingled. But Mother, well that's a different story!"

That very evening after work Ted stopped at the corner store and picked up a newspaper. He turned to the classifieds and scrolled through the rentals. *Aha, here's just the place. Four bedrooms, one bath, living room, dining room, kitchen, screened porch.* The next day, Sunday, Ted hopped a bus for Arlington Heights where the house was located. The place appeared to be in good condition and even had a small fenced backyard. He went to a phone booth, called the number listed and made an appointment. The owner said he would meet him within the hour.

Ted walked around the area. There was a small grocery store on the corner. *That's convenient*, he thought. He made another phone call.

"Uncle Ed, this is Ted. I'm over on Highland Avenue looking at a rental property. No, for the family. Yes. I have an appointment to see it today but I just walked around and it looks pretty good. Nice neighborhood. Close to the trolley too. Okay, I'll let you know. Bye."

"If the rent is reasonable, I'll take it right away. That should solve the problem of Caroline and Thomas," said Ted aloud.

The owner introduced himself as he and Ted shook hands. "Come on in, I'll show you around. The former tenants just bought a house so the place is vacant. I want to spruce it up a bit before I rent it. You're the first to see it."

They climbed the three wide steps to the covered porch in front. The owner put the key in the lock. As Ted stepped inside he had a feeling of *déjà vu*. It reminded him of his home in Halifax. This looks great, thought Ted. They agreed on the rent, starting the first of September.

Ted was elated. Now the family could be together. Instead of phoning his uncle, he decided to take the bus directly to the shipyards. Uncle Ed was pleased that Ted found something so quickly. "Does that mean you'll be moving out? Aunt Sally will be heartbroken but we'll understand."

"I'm not sure. I'd like to get the family settled first. I like living here but I don't know. I haven't thought about myself."

Ted telephoned his mother after dinner that night. "Mother, how are you? Are you enjoying your summer?"

Martha didn't want her son to know that she was miserable. Their summer place had been such a part of her husband; it didn't seem right without him. Besides she missed both men. "I'm just fine, dear."

"I miss you, and the kids too." He hesitated. "Mother, how would you like to move to the States? I found a really nice place to rent. Reminds me of our house on Quimpool Road. I know you'd love it and it'd be nice to have everyone together. The rent is quite reasonable and is available the first of September."

"Oh dear, September? Then that means the children would have to register for school there, wouldn't it? My goodness, this is a lot to think about."

Martha stopped for a moment. "Ted, this has been a hard summer for us. We miss you and Dad and it just seems there's so much work to do. It's rained nearly every day and the mosquitoes are vicious. The States sounds like a nice change for us. The kids have moped about this summer. It just isn't the same." Her voice caught in her throat.

"Okay then it's settled. You break the news to everyone and I'll see about getting passage for all of you. I'll call you in a few days."

"Thank you, dear. Thank you. Bye."

"Mother seemed relieved about coming to the States," he told his aunt and uncle. "I don't think she likes being at Summerhill without Dad. And maybe she's concerned about the children even though she didn't say so."

"I'm happy for you, Ted," said Aunt Sally. "I'll bet your uncle can help you get tickets for them to come by ship."

"Of course, of course," said Ed. "Let's see. You want them to be here on the first of September? I'll check tomorrow and let you know."

"Great. And thanks to you both. I know I'll be happy if they are closer to me. I still feel responsible and worry about them."

The last week of August came quickly. At last the family was ready. They set sail on the SS Prince George. The tickets were ten dollars apiece and they were able to take several crates containing their belongings, even some furniture. However, the weather was cold and rainy and the Bay of Fundy was extremely rough. Many passengers were seasick and were a sorry sight when they finally arrived in Boston and passed through immigrations. But once safely on land they felt better. The first off the ship was Allan, who literally flew into his brother's arms.

"Welcome to the United States," said Ted, hugging him tightly.

"We were all sick. I didn't know if we'd make it. You should see all the stuff we brought with us...suitcases, two trunks, and furniture."

Ted smiled. He sounded so much like Caroline who always tried to get everything into one sentence. He hugged him again. "I'm glad you're here. I'm really glad you all are here at last. Look at you, Caroline. Oh my, you've become a beautiful young lady. And Jerry, I think you are taller than me. How did that happen?" He went to hug Jerry but shook the outstretched hand instead.

"Mother, I'm so happy to see you." He hugged her long and hard then looked around. "Where's Grandma?" Just then, Grandma appeared holding the hands of Charles and Elizabeth. "I don't believe it. You've all grown so much."

He picked up Charles. Elizabeth came running over to him. "Me too," she said. as Ted scooped her up in his other arm. "Welcome to the States. You don't know how happy I am to see you. There's nothing like family together."

Epilogue

Within thirty minutes of the Halifax Explosion on December 6, 1917, search and rescue parties were organized and at work among the wreckage, digging out the dead and injured. By four o'clock that afternoon, the city fire department had the ship blaze under control and a mere twelve hours later most fires were out except for a few isolated and contained areas, but the debris continued to smolder and burn for days.

1,963 estimated killed

9,000 injured, with 199 blinded

1,600 buildings destroyed, 12,000 more damaged

$35 million loss of property

2,600 tons of explosives

There were so many people admitted to Victoria General that they lost count. In their wild panic, the people of Halifax fled their homes and stores. They left them unguarded and unlocked. In no time, looters were at work turning over the wreckage and rifling corpses.

The immediate task was to provide aid for the injured, shelter for the homeless and food for the hungry. Offers of money and relief came pouring in, not only from other parts of Canada but also from all over the world.

New Zealand made a grant of $50,000

Australia sent $250,000

London opened a fund that closed at $600,000

The generosity of many countries was great, but it was from the United States of America that the first and most valuable assistance came. By nine o'clock Thursday night a special train from Boston arrived with a large quantity of medical supplies followed by a second train the following day with doctors, nurses and orderlies and carrying equipment for a 500 bed hospital.

Also, a relief train from New York City arrived several days later laden with cots, clothing, blankets, and cases of disinfectant.

Help came from all over America. It came by rail and it came by sea. Altogether the contributions amounted to close to $30,000,000.

New York held a special Halifax Relief Day raising $75,000

Chicago cabled $130,000

Boston sent a steamer with supplies valued at $150,000

The people of Halifax have never forgotten the most generous and spontaneous aid. In appreciation, each year a huge Christmas tree is sent to Boston, the first to be lighted for the season.

As for the O'Neill family, they settled in Massachusetts. Attending the tree lighting became yet another tradition for the O'Neills, a celebration of their old and new lives.

Once the children were in school, Martha took a job as a school nurse while Grandma ran the household.

Upon graduation from high school, Caroline won a scholarship to Massachusetts Art School and later taught in the public school system. After college, Jerry taught history in a private school. Allan apprenticed under Ted and developed a keen eye for jewelry design. Charles, also artistic, won many awards for his paintings and later became a commercial artist in California. Elizabeth studied ballet but chose marriage and raising a family over a career.

Ted was successful as a jeweler and watchmaker and eventually opened a second shop managed by his brother, Allan. Ted married Anna and together they produced seven children.

This novel is a tribute to my father, Ted O'Neill, a kind and generous man. My family, as did many families, survived and grew through their tragedies. It was a matter of time.

TIME

Time, where does it go
Does anyone know
Does it fly away on gossamer wings
Is it disguised as a bird that sings

Does anyone know
How does it flow
Is it disguised as a bird that sings
It could be any one of these things

How does it flow
I really don't know
It could be any one of these things
Does it sound like a bell that gongs or rings

I really don't know
It doesn't show
Does it sound like a bell that gongs or rings
Or is it soft like a flowing spring

It doesn't show
Does it fly away on gossamer wings
Or is it soft like a flowing spring
Time, where does it go

A pantoum by Diane O'Neill DesRochers